I DO SO WORRY FOR ALL THOSE LOST AT SEA

An Imagined Autobiography
by
David Keyes

THE HOUSE OF POMEGRANATES PRESS

WWW.HOUSEOFPOMEGRANATES.COM

Published by The House of Pomegranates Press
www.houseofpomegranates.ca

ISBN 978-0-9784543-4-0

For Gillian

Preface

WHEN THE TIME came to print a second edition of this book, we took the opportunity to add a few extras in the hopes of making it even more magical than the original.

A new story, *Mr. Flowers Talks To The Dead*, a secret chapter which was not included in the original edition, has been added to this volume.

When the first edition of the book was published, we commissioned our friend Richard Shallhorn to concoct martini recipes suitable for Mr. P, which we printed as a small book to give away at the launch party. *The 5 Cocktails of Mr. P* proved so popular, not to mention delicious, that we decided to include them here for your enjoyment.

On the cover of this second edition is a most wonderful and haunting painting by Ray Caesar. We would like to thank Mr. Caesar for his kind permission to use this image.

Contents

The House of Sleep

PUTTING EMILY TO bed, a small nightlight casts fantastic shadows about the warm room. Her angel wings hang upon the door.

"William, I am writing a novel."

"Are you? Of what?"

"Of the people who live in this house."

"You and me?"

"No, silly, not us. I'm writing about the other people who live here."

She yawns, kisses me. "Goodnight William. I love you."

I SHOULD TELL you this before I begin. My family — all — suffered from narcolepsy and we would find ourselves falling asleep at the most inopportune moments. I say this not to betray my family as in any way odd, though in our way we were, but to let you know just how deep our sleep could be.

Chapter 1

IT IS EARLY in the evening, Halloween night, and I have walked out to our gate, an umbrella in one hand and a cup of tea in the other. The air tonight is cool and wet, made more so by our closeness to the sea and the dense forests that shoulder us on either side. The sky is rippled with clouds and, shivering somewhere behind them and our house, is the moon. I am dressed in a burgundy smoking jacket, baggy black trousers and a pair of rather large Wellingtons that I took from the enormous array of boots, walking sticks, hats and gloves that lie rumpled and piled upon the great hallstand. My father bought the stand one autumn at a local church jumble sale, attracted I think by its strange mixture of hooks and drawers. Made of mahogany, it has an oval mirror that reflects everything in a soupy ghost-like manner and giant lion's paw feet that thrust out to trip up anyone who gets too close. The jacket belonged to my father as I suspect did the Wellingtons, for he was slightly larger than I and far more dapper.

My father was an inventor. He owned the patent on a number of clever devices that to this day have not been made obsolete, and this generated an income that he used to finance his true love, spiritualism; his books were nearly all dedicated to it. He was, I suspect, trying to contact his father who had disappeared off the coast one night and was never heard from again. My father took this quite hard and dedicated his free hours, when not with us, to the matter.

My mother was a botanist — an evoker of flowers my father called her — and a patron saint to the bees who came here uninvited and never left, their industriousness mirroring hers. Through their partnership strains of flowers were born, many bearing my sister's name or mine. The bees are asleep now, their hives silent, their consciousness slumbering. If you place a hand gently upon the chilly wooden frames you can feel the dreams blanketing the hive like an electrical field. How she would shudder if she saw the state of her garden now; the greenhouse my father built for her is dark and covered in lichen and all along the path vines and branches reach out yearning for her gentle touch. The orchard, whose lovely petals used to turn the drive pink each spring, has all but disappeared and the maze, once so symmetrical and serene, is now frightening and overgrown, full of foxes and spider webs.

The house itself is made of buttery stone with jutting spires and a gray slate roof. Over there is my bedroom. It was my father's favourite room and I love it the most. It has the highest ceilings in the whole of the house with huge windows that open up onto a view of the lawn and the quite sudden drop from the cliff to the sea crashing below. It had originally been refurbished while my parents were on their honeymoon; two downstairs rooms had been annexed and opened up to some of the servant's quarters above. Although it was meant to be their bedroom, they slept in it only once. Their first night back my mother, frightfully ill from food poisoning, saw my dead grandfather covered in seaweed thumb through a book and then leave through a panel by the fireplace. After fitfully vomiting upon my startled father, she cried out what she had seen and never entered the room again. Another master bedroom was established and the first one became my father's library, where in his not very idle hours he would attempt to receive the spirit world. When I moved in — well aware of the myth of my grandfather and the fireplace — I spent days searching but found nothing save a doorknob behind a row of Arthur Conan Doyles, that opened to a forgotten dumb-waiter.

Sadly, the house's days as a family house ended with the loss of my sister, whose passing was like a high watermark upon the walls. From then on things could not carry on as they had. Except for the care of her daughter, my niece Emily, I thought of nothing else but to grow old with the house. Even when I did not happen to look upon a mirror, I could still see in the worn carpets and faded curtains just how shabby and uncared for I had become.

Tonight though, with its lights ablaze, the house

looks almost happy. Tonight it is my birthday, tonight I turn 31 and tonight Emily has arranged a party.

Chapter 2

FORGIVE ME.

I have since my childhood been haunted by a recurring dream. I am out at sea. It is black. No stars. No sound. There is a sensation of warmth or cold but I am never sure which. I am aware of being in a boat that rocks gently beneath me. I am calm. Slowly it lightens and the sea around me becomes visible. It is purple — a rich aubergine cloth that undulates gently around the boat.

I am standing as the sea billows while slivers of diamond light shower around me. Suddenly above me I see a crown — mediaeval, simple, beautiful — I reach up and try to take hold of it but it seems to be slightly higher than my reach. As I stand and stretch to my full height, my fingers so close, it floats higher; it's as if the crown and I are like magnetic poles, so the space between us stays always the same. I'm never frustrated, even after a lifetime of this. The sea then turns dark and the dream ends as it began, fading slowly to black, and I awake.

Since I began having this dream I have always dreamed of myself as an adult, at the age I am now. I have noticed that as I get older, I become more aware of the surroundings and now try to take note consciously when I can. On the floor of the boat, for example, there are smallish animals — rabbits, hamsters, hedgehogs — but I am not sure if they have always been there. I have sniffed the air and noticed that it smells of talc. Other times I have looked to the surrounding inky horizon but have seen nothing hidden there in its shadows, just the purple sea spanning out. What I have found though, and this disturbs me greatly, is that I am starting to see people within the waves. I had always thought that the sea was solid yet now and then, just breaking the surface like a fish, a hand or face has appeared.

I always wake slightly edgy, and this invariably sets my mood for the entire day.

Chapter 3

ALTHOUGH NARCOLEPTIC, I was from time to time cursed with a dreadful insomnia and would often wander the house late at night while my family slept. There was a room that faced out across the lawns where I would sit and wait for the moon to come into view then begin its slow descent behind the trees. In the summer, very late at night, I would often see my sister coming out of the forest that bordered the lawn, gracefully leaving a trail on the silver dew-covered grass.

There was never a point in my life when I did not consider my sister beautiful. She was tall and slender with long velvety black hair and skin the colour of cream. Even from an early age she did nothing unintentionally and as she aged, she grew silent and introspective. I remember her best sitting for hours beneath the shade of the willows on our front lawn. When we were children we were equal in mind and body, hungrily sharing experiences as children growing up in a world of adults are wont to do. However, when she began to exhibit signs — when she'd fall asleep or disappear for hours, showing up wet, speechless and distraught — she began the process of distancing herself from the family. We had all believed that she had not inherited our illness and when it did finally begin to show I think it hit her hard. To her it was less a quirk to be nervously laughed off and more an omen — something feared and not to be taken lightly.

My bedroom back then was on the third floor of the house. You could climb out the window onto the roof of the library below and if brave enough continue down to the ground via the ancient ivy that twisted and tangled itself against the side. One July night, when the air was floating heavy and warm with the scent of the cooling lawns and flowers, my sister quite unexpectedly climbed through the window. She had obviously been in the woods and was naked, glistening with perspiration and forest dew and flecked with drying salt. This was the first time I had seen her body this close since I was little and it made me uncomfortable. The black of her hair so contrasted against her pale skin. She settled in beside me, pulled her feet up and pushed into me for warmth. She was clammy and cold and I put my arm around her uneasily. She put her head on my chest, her long hair spilling down. I thought, this is how someone feels who has drowned.

"Do you think we will live forever?" she whispered to me. "I mean, forever?"

"I don't think so. I hope not. I don't think I would like that," I said, staring forward at the trees. Within their darkness, swarming fireflies made their own twinkling cosmos. "Do you want to live forever?" I asked her. She curled closer. "I know I won't. I know we won't but I just don't want this to end. I know we should eventually want to move away but I feel as if we've all been placed here for a reason. Mummy and Daddy always seemed more misguided curators than parents. Do you know what Daddy said when I fell down the stairs, when I was ten and broke my arm? Do you? He said that if I must fall, I should try harder to do it down the carpeted stairs. I loved him. I loved them. I love you. I don't want this summer, this evening, this feeling as if I am about to burst, to end." She took my palm and examined it, putting her finger upon a line. "See," she said, "none of us are here for long."

"I feel the same way but I also feel somewhat smothered by the ghosts and the fact that we are bound together not only by blood but by sleep and ..." I trailed off.

"I'm pregnant."

"What? Pregnant? Are you joking? You never leave the grounds. How can you be pregnant?"

"I've just decided," she said. She shifted, pushing a strand of hair away from her face. I felt a gentle pressure from her breast against my arm. "Here," she took my hand and placed it on her stomach. "Feel. It's a girl. I am going to call her Emily. She will be just like us, but she won't."

"You're insane," I said, moving my hand away. "Who is the father? Are you sure?"

"Of course I'm sure," she said, looking at me clearly and with terrifying seriousness. "I am the father. The house is her father. The dreams that swirl within fathered her. The notes we write, the books we leave upturned, the places we go when we are asleep, the shadows that climb the walls at night, the trees swishing, the sea and tides, the moon. They are all her father and when I am gone, I want you to love her more than..."

"Stop!" I pleaded. "I don't want to know this. I love you and never question you, but I don't want to know!"

"We are all going to die, William. You said so yourself. Some sooner, some later, but we are all going to die. With Emily I am moving forward in another form and you have to promise," and she took my hand and placed it back on her stomach, "you will always watch out for her."

And as she said that, almost imperceptibly, I felt a slight movement inside of her.

Chapter 4

EMILY HAS ARRANGED the party for me tonight and in her excitement has fallen asleep on the huge couch in my father's study. She is wearing the bunny costume she now refuses to be without and looks so lost and heart-breakingly frail as she sleeps. The fire is low and orange and shadows grow and fall upon the walls. Within the shadows there are other shadows, shape shifters and spirits running rife within the wallpaper's patterns. Glass-covered cases line two of the walls and are filled with Joan of Arc trial transcripts, spiritualism texts, alchemic essays, editions of Alice in Wonderland and also odd bits of stone from numerous family trips, all labeled minute-ly in my father's hand. Added to this are Emily's tiny sailboats, dolls and bits of sea glass, which each day she rearranges, the taxonomy known only to her. I have often stumbled upon her — this serious little girl in her bunny costume — whispering to herself, meticulously arrang-ing her collection. Around the room, paper and books are stacked on the carpeted floor and, almost lost beside the thick curtains, a monkey skeleton, jauntily wearing a fez, lurks near the window. During family disagreements my father would speak directly to him, calling him Basil.

In the centre of the room is a tiny stage-set my sister made for Emily. It is lit by an odd system of lights and at times when the house is still and silent it almost seems to pulse with a life of its own. It is a miniature of the room we are in now with tiny pasteboard cutouts of Emily, me and my sister. Although I have rarely seen her do it, this too seems to change each day. For a while my sister's cutout disappeared. I asked Emily where it went and she said quite fervently, "Away." So inside the cardboard room my cutout and hers mourned alone. At times I found my paper self on its back behind the tiny couch (was she saying I drink too much?), while Emily's seemed to move from the bookcase to the window seat then back again. Sometimes she was placed upside-down, at other times in my paper arms. Then last year just before my birthday the paper cutout of my sister reappeared standing beside mine, looking out the blank window. I asked Emily about this reoccurrence and she explained earnestly, "Mommy is here now. You just can't see her."

Of all the rooms in the house, this has become hers more than any other — this was where my father and his spiritualist chums conducted their séances, this is where they spoke to the spirit world and this, I suspect, is where my father now speaks directly to her. From here, you cannot hear the sea.

List of folders in my father's filing cabinet:

As Yet Un-invented Items
14th Century Farming
Newt Rearing
Stars, Planets and Their Relation to Cookery
Wines
What I Have Gotten Right
What I have Gotten Wrong
Carnivorous Plants and their Uses
Poisons
Possible Novel Ideas

Chapter 5

MY SISTER SAT away from the sun under the willows. We had just come down from school. The weather that day was languid and soft, the sea a constant aquamarine. As I approached, her cat Nathaniel mewed slightly. Without looking up from her book, she reached out and stroked him quietly. Moving closer the cat settled and began to purr, its eyes closing slightly.

"I think sometimes," she said, putting her book down and looking up at me, "our family is like that suitcase Joseph Cornell made Marcel Duchamp. Have you heard of it?"

"Joseph Cornell used to follow shop girls around New York on their lunch breaks." I said.

She frowned at me then continued, "He filled it full of things. Crazy things like bits of paper and scraps of letters with words underlined and ticket stubs. You could dump everything out and try to make sense of it but it wasn't like a puzzle that had borders and matching pieces. There was or wasn't a reason for everything. I look at our lives here," she glanced past me towards the house, Nathaniel following her gaze, "and I think 'what does it mean?' Us. Our bizarre world."

I just shrugged and lay down on the warm grass beside her.

Chapter 6

WE WERE DRUNK. My sister and I had stolen wine from the kitchen and had been drinking all night. She was losing at cards, something she hated to do, and gathering Nathaniel and her glass had stormed out, slamming the door petulantly behind her. I walked about my room touching the indentations she had made and righting objects she had moved. Finding one of her hairs, long and black, I laid it carefully in my book. I could hear my heart beat. The clock chimed three. Outside moonlight shifted the trees.

Then I heard it. Faintly. I crept over and opened the door. My father was in the hall pushing the drinks cart, the bottles jostling on top like a tiny drunken bell choir. He was sleepwalking. I half wanted to laugh and yet was scared at seeing my father led solely by his subconscious. He paused and not really seeing me stepped forward and whispered, "This house has seventeen rooms, with seventeen doors and seventeen floors." He looked around conspiratorially and said, "I will take you there, if you want me to. I will take you there." Elegantly bowing, he then stepped back and resumed pushing the cart towards the end of the hall.

That was the last time I saw my father.

Chapter 7

THE FOREST BESIDE our house is so dense it seems forever in darkness, the ground always wet and soft and green. Deep inside the gloom there is a circular clearing where the trees surround — like a wall — a small stone quarry; their branches finger above to provide shade so it is never too hot, never too sunny and always awash in lovely filtered green light. There is never a breeze and sounds are muffled and stilled. When we were little my sister and I would play there almost daily, but as we grew older we frequented it less and less. When I was old enough to go away to school, I stopped going there all together and it retreated into memory as yet another haunted place from my childhood. I had thought my sister had done the same as she never mentioned it to me; however, sometimes late at night watching her cross the lawn, I suspected that was where she was coming from.

Chapter 8

PICKING EMILY UP from the couch, I notice that she is becoming as beautiful as her mother was. She weighs nothing, her pink costume glowing in the dark. Walking back through the house and out onto the terrace, I see Mr. P in fancy dress out on the black lawn trying to light little Japanese paper lanterns.

Mr. P is our neighbour to the north. He had been a close friend of my parents and would often visit for dinner parties. Although he was a wolf, he stood upright using a cane and had the most beautiful silver-gray fur. He smelled of moss and earth, as if he had just come from some gloriously lush garden where he had been rolling about. In the summer he wore huge baggy shorts with a hole at the back for his tail and a white dress shirt with the sleeves rolled up. He had vaguely human hands and although my parents taught me it was the very height of impoliteness to stare, I always marveled at the complex choreography he used to grasp the most minute of objects. He had a liking for vodka and cranberry juice with just a dash of Cointreau, and was a vegetarian. "Like Shaw," he would say.

He was a cartographer. His desire was to be known just for his map-making and his charting so we tried as much as possible to talk of that and not of his wolf past (although I know my father was privy to at least some of his secrets, as they had been roommates at college). His talent was that of an interpretive cartographer; he would use his senses rather than science to transcribe the geography of a place. His work was so detailed and evocative it would often wind up framed on walls rather than dog-eared from use and stored in long flat drawers. In my mother's room there is an extraordinary topographical survey of her pumpkin patch that he gave her one autumn. He also mapped our two houses. So obsessive was he that along with the plumbing, electrical wires, furniture and fixtures, he also included the placement of the pictures and the contents of the shelves, drawers and closets; there is even a map of the mouse holes. He mapped the forest that divided our properties and the disused tunnels that joined them, including the one that led out to the sea. And he mapped the sea itself.

I know my mother adored him and would often send over flowers or the first pickings of strawberries. I remember coming upon an evening of bridge and seeing my mother gently stroking his ear, Mr. P's eyes rolling slightly, while my father talked of the railway. My sister and I also adored him. He was our godparent (though my parents were in no way religious except regarding cocktail hour) and he always remembered our birthdays, giving us tiny pencil sets and blank books and once, some small magical instruments used to dowse for water. In the summer he would take us for long walks, knowing how at times our parents were preoccupied with their work. We would stroll around our land or down to the sea, Mr. P in striped swimming trunks with a black parasol held high above his head.

Though he loved us and loved being around us, somewhere in his eyes there was always a certain sadness which betrayed his jovial manner; they seemed to say that 'although my talents are great and my friends many I will never really fit in'. Often at night after a visit my sister and I would wonder at the origin of this melancholy. Certainly a lot had to do with the fact that it was awkward for him simply to go out. He would not eat in restaurants, buy a loaf of bread or go to the cinema in town as there was always that fear of startling someone new, so he kept to himself even though all the people in the village knew and loved him (and some of the most useful maps in the town hall were his). In our early teens my sister and I developed the theory that he and our mother had been, at some point, lovers. We had even decided that he had moved here, to the house connected by hidden tunnels, just to be close to her — a wolf Gatsby standing on his lawn, his keen sense of hearing searching out her laughter in the night air. But whatever his reason for being here, he was amusing and refined and as a guest at dinner was always witty and wonderfully, charmingly magical.

Although he is still a great friend to me, he rarely visits. Though we never speak of it, Emily has a relationship with him far more spiritual than my sister and I ever did, in spite of the fact that he became like a father to us when our parents disappeared, and stayed with us while we waited for some word. To help pass the awful hours he would take us for drives in his car, the wonderfully romantically named *Shooting Drake*. While driving he told us of his school days and his travels, though we wondered how true they were, as we had never seen him venture any farther than to town and only then by night. I think that once my parents vanished and my sister disappeared, once this house fell into disarray, he wanted to keep the memory of my family as we were when we were all here and happy. I have always suspected that for him time is infinite but while once it passed pleasurably, it now treads with heavy steps.

Emily stirs and jumps down from my arms, running down the stairs and out onto the sodden grass. She gleefully throws herself at Mr. P who falls to the ground and is instantly soaked. Righting himself and laughing almost as loud as Emily, he picks her up in his great arms and holds her high in the air. She hugs his silver head and he gently licks the tip of her nose with his long wolf tongue, just as he used to do with my sister and me. He places her back on the grass and bending, speaks quietly to her. She then suddenly darts away to the trees, full of energy.

"Emily, not at night," I call out, forever afraid of the darkness of the forest. She pays no heed and soon returns holding the hand of Mrs. Z, who is dressed in a deep blue Victorian bathing costume with her black hair hanging loosely over her shoulders. She has an unlit Japanese lantern suspended from the end of a pole that she dangles near Mr. P, who, bowing, lights the candle within. Emily then runs to another tree and disappears behind it only to emerge with Mr. H, our neighbour to the west, his brown rabbit features catching the light from the newly lit lanterns. He lets go of Emily to adjust his jacket and gloves, running his hands along his whiskers and enormous ears. He, too, seems to be dressed in Victorian attire and suddenly I no longer feel the outsider standing there with my neighbours, all misfits, moving in the glow of the paper lanterns.

Emily runs back and forth, making sure Mr. P has dry matches, and Mrs. Z makes it safely across the lawn, then over to me and finally back to talk to Mr. H. "Yes, yes," I hear from the shrubbery beside the terrace. There is a rumble of thunder. Mr. P looks up at the sky, waving a match. Emily then runs back to me. "Happy Birthday William."

"Thank you Emily, how wonderful. What are you and Mr. H up to?" I ask.

"He has brought the O sisters to do a pantomime for us. I had wanted them to come dancing out of the woods but it seems they are late," she sighs.

"Hallo!" shouts Mr. H pointing to the side of the house, "the sisters cometh."

Mrs. Z claps her hands joyously as Mr. P straightens his back and from behind the house run the two O sisters with a great sense of urgency, dressed in Victorian undergarments and speaking as one. "Sorry, sorry, sorry. We had to stop to put up the roof of the car. Oh," noticing the lanterns, "how magical! Emily, you are a magician," and they both reach for her, bundling her in a sea of dancerly flesh and pantaloons.

"How wonderful to see you all," I say. Another clap of thunder and suddenly the rain starts to fall. Everyone dashes for the terrace door. "Careful, the stones are slippery. Hurry inside."

What a strange and wonderful parade we make: Emily in her bunny suit followed by Mrs. Z in her bathing costume and the still-lit lantern on a stick, Mr. P, his fur bristling from the electrical storm followed by the sisters all white and ribbons and grace, and then Mr. H, who rubs his hands together then gently slaps me upon the back. "Happy Birthday, William. I trust this will be a magical evening for us all. I'm sorry your sister couldn't be here. She would have loved this, loved it all."

"Yes," I said, ushering him in and closing the door, silencing the storm behind us. "She would have loved it."

Chapter 9

"THAT YEAR WAS the most pleasant," Father said to my sister and me, unprovoked, facing the window, holding a cocktail, seeming very far away. "In Mr. P I found someone to share my digs and conversation. Charming, so charming and so intelligent on all manner of topics, with none of that painful politics of youth. I was also proud of my new friend; how decent he was; how intelligent and wise, how silent and caring. It was a year of intense study and growing. We were misfits, mind you — misfits of misfits I think it's fair to say — so we gained a reputation for being eccentrics in a place where eccentricities generally go unnoticed. That was something to be proud of," Father punctuated, poking Basil the monkey skeleton.

"I remember one time we were drowsy, and I suggested we head to the shops. I needed this and that and I had found something in a little out-of-the-way shop that I wanted to show Mr. P most urgently. Like everyone in Oxford we rode bicycles. What a pair we were." Again, he poked Basil.

"Presently we came upon a small shop in an out-of-the-way cul de sac, with a large tree in the center. Under that was an ornate bench with a brass plaque that read, *Curiouser and Curiouser*. I turned to old P and said that I'd found this in one of my wanderings. We did that, find secrets to share. Became a game almost. I had quite lost my way, I said, and found this ancient shop. It looked all Tudor; in the crossbeams were carved fish and skulls."

"A fish monger doctor?" asked Mr. P.

The sign above the door said *Curiosities*.

"I remember Mr. P saying, 'What better place for the likes of us?'

"The shop seemed lightless, airless when we entered, a musty sort of gloom; sunlight was unable to penetrate the greasy front windows, the only sound was all the ticking clocks. There was a hunched man with a green cellulose visor sitting behind a glass cabinet, with a loupe in one eye, poking at a very small box with a screwdriver. When he saw us, he put the box down and beamed."

Father mimicked the accent, " 'Gentlemen, please, welcome to my humble shop. I have seen you before, have I not?' he said to me, extending his hand.

"Yes, I was in last week and asked you to hold a certain item for my friend."

" 'Of course, of course, this is your lupine friend? How wonderful. Marvelous to meet you. Cartography, you see,' and in a flourish he reached up and with a stick pulled down a beautifully detailed map of the Indian Ocean, 'is a passion of mine. You sir, if you will forgive me, are making waves in the college. Perhaps I can introduce you to a colleague of mine at the Society, he may have a commission.' Then he paused, cleared his throat, 'Forgive me. Please, I will fetch the item you have come to see. I put it away for safekeeping. There is so much more to see in the store. Please,' he said gesturing, 'browse. You can never visit the same shop twice. Everything changes here so quickly. You have it at the moment to yourselves, save for a rather gloomy American gentleman who has wandered off to the back.' Switching on a lamp, he gestured for us to explore.

"The shop was difficult to navigate, as if the Natural History Museum backed its lorry up to the front door and dumped. And it was damned warm and snug, and smelled of lemon and wood and dust. Everything looked as if it was a sepia-tinted mystery. Bowls of glass door-knobs, exotic collections of alchemic devices; books with gold pentagrams covers that read 'Investigative Mysteries'; cabinets after cabinets filled with jars of liquid, candles, and Victorian miscellany, hair pictures, jet. 'Look at this deck of cards,' I said, as they slowly rose into the air, each card with a girl on it or a hand gesture or a phrase.

'What kind of place is this?' asked P.

"The shopkeeper suddenly appeared. 'Gentlemen?' He had in his arms a box covered with tissue that probably, at one time, contained roses. 'I believe this is what you were looking for.'

" 'P,' I said, 'I found this when I was here last. I think you will like it.'

'May I?' said P.

'Of course,' said the shopkeeper.

'Good lord, is it…?'

"I said, 'I've never seen one so life-like, I found it for you.'

'My best friend,' said P and gently pulled out a perfectly articulated arm and hand. Wires and gears hung from its stump as if it had been wrenched off the owner's body quite violently. The arm was that of a woman, delicate and long. Her wrist was thin, the fingers splayed out, each joint movable. You should have seen him, he was dumb-struck; he turned it over again and again. Then the shop owner reached over and pulled at one of the dangling wires and the hand clasped. 'Oh goodness,' said P. 'This is almost too sad.'

'Look,' I said, 'she has a tattoo.'

"The shopkeeper said, 'She has no record, no recorded history. She is an orphan. A gentleman brought her in, sold her to me, wanted nothing to do with her. Said he found her in an old trunk resting in straw. He wanted cash. I cannot think who could have manufactured her. There is generally a mark or a date; I can find nothing. By the mechanics, the skin colour, the ring on her finger, I can date her almost to the year. 1810, say, but her country of origin…Germany? Austria? Who is she?' he whispered. 'Did she play the piano? She could have with that kind of mechanics, but where is the rest of her? Ah, it is a delicious mystery, no?'

"P whispered, 'I must have this.'

"The owner smiled. 'I will leave you to consider and please, as I said, browse. Many things have changed since last you were here. I have nothing but time.' And he bowed, backing away.

" 'This is so marvelous," said P. 'I can't believe you

found such a thing here… in this shop… in this city… here.'

" 'It is marvelous and if I had the ready cash I would buy it for you.'

" 'No… no… thank you my dear friend. I have cash and I must have this.'

"I remember we were so lost in the arm, in the moment we didn't notice the American who was wandering the store with us, picking up objects and putting them back. I see him so clearly; he was a thickset man with wiry black hair and olive skin. He seemed all muscle: burly, barrel-chested, small. There was a sadness to his face and his slow, methodical actions. He looked lost. He was dressed in a maroon wool suit, completely unsuitable for the warmish Spring day. He held a bowler hat in his hand, which looked new, and he turned it round and round by the rim.

"There was a large spiritualist disappearing cabinet that the American was fascinated with. He ran his hand along the dark, gleaming, lacquered wood. Inside someone had placed a small padded stool. He pulled the velvet curtain fully back and sat down. We, now aware of him, turned and introduced ourselves. He sat in the cabinet dejectedly, as if caught up quite suddenly with fatigue.

"There was a basket of cutlery beside the cabinet, sets of forks or spoons, all tied in blue silk ribbon; he poked the basket with his foot and smiled and said, 'Have you noticed the North American…not say, the drawing room North American with European pretensions but the real American, cultured in their own way…how they eat? Compared to the English, there is a hesitance. Using both hands but not in unison. The left, or the right on the fork with the other hand dead at the side or under the table or on a glass; ready to catch something that has fallen or to scratch a dog's ear. Crossing back and forth, knife to fork. Uncertain. Alone. The English however, have confidence. They rule double-fisted over their plate. Knife firmly in one hand, fork in the other. Plowing and cultivating their food as if they had a God-given right to walk the fields as if they owned them. I believe they have a love of eating — the pantomime, the dance — but not a love of taste, as English food is bland and horrendous; for that is too sensual, and the English are not sensual. That act of pushing the food up onto the backs of their forks. The English love only what they own and guard it jealously like a stubborn spouse refusing a divorce. Any interesting taste they come across they must conquer and debase!'

"And then he pulled the cabinet's curtain shut and I swear to you, he disappeared."

Father then drank down his cocktail and said, "Argh, warm, terrible stuff when warm."

Chapter 10

MY SISTER WAS returning from her first and only year at boarding school and I had been sent to fetch her in Mr. P's car, driven by his man, Mr. Flowers. The sky that day was bluer than blue, cornflower blue, and the countryside was filled with islands of daffodils that seemed to be floating in light green seas. New ivy grew on the rock walls that closely lined the road towards the station, a bizarre cottage-like structure with ornate gardens and gables and a white picket fence.

I stood in the cool shade of the platform and waited, the huge clock that hung down like a thought-bubble, clicking away the minutes. Without warning the stationmaster shot out from some unseen door holding his florescent paddle and wearily eyeing the distant horizon. "A bit late," he muttered to me. There was no direct train from or to the city so one had to transfer seven times, and with each transfer the conveyance got smaller and smaller, the last being a tiny three-car coach with wooden doors on either side and a black engine that looked like an angry teapot, which sighed and banked when it turned, going around hills rather than through them.

A plume of smoke and a sharp whistle in the distance announced its arrival and from around the bend it ambled in, listing to one side on the curve then righting itself and stopping at the platform with a huge steam sigh. The stationmaster went from door to door with a tiny stool helping people to alight, and from a 3rd class carriage the doors flew open and my sister jumped down. Pulling her things out of the car she turned and spotted me and, dropping her bags, ran down the platform. "William!" she cried and threw her arms around me. "Promise me... promise me that you will never let them send me back. I will die if I have to spend another year with those adenoidal, horsy girls. We must petition Mummy and Daddy, we must! Oh I am so glad to be home. Is Nathaniel...?" and she picked me up and spun me around, and then, in our excitement, we crumpled onto the platform floor, brother and sister in a narcoleptic trance. The stationmaster, quite used to our family by now, placed my sister's cases beside us and, shutting the last of the train's doors, blew his whistle and sent the little train trudging on.

Chapter 11

THE HOUSE TO the west had been empty for years. It was a vast, unloved and windy place, and my sister and I had spent many a day imagining a tragic and mysterious history for it — blood would ooze nightly from every crevice; lights were seen and voices heard while shadowy figures walked the roof; depressions in the rolling, unkempt lawn were actually undetected Burmese tiger traps. Then one spring day a caravan of vehicles rolled up to the shackled gate. From its size and shape, my sister and I were convinced that a circus troop had rented out the house and we rushed across the lawn to the hedgerows to spy.

An elegant, elongated car headed the parade. Behind it were vans of all shapes filled with what we were sure to be tents and elephants, freaks and clowns. To our delight, a rather well-dressed and seemingly gigantic hare emerged from the car. He was dressed in black and on his hands were white leather driving gloves. He walked up to the rusted gate with its ancient lichen-covered *To Let* sign, pulled a key out of his waistcoat pocket and inserted it in to the lock, which crumbled to dust as he touched it. He gave the enormous gate a shove. At first it did not budge. He applied his weight a second time until it finally gave way and swung in, creaking so loudly that hordes of startled birds took to the sky, filling it with shadows. He looked back at the caravan then got in his car and drove on. Like a procession of ants, the rest followed — trucks and vans and an ancient horse-drawn hearse, the horses proud and apparently used to parading. We were bursting with excitement and ran to the house to tell our parents. My father was in his study, lost in some sort of three-dimensional algebra. When we told him that a circus troop led by a hare had just moved in next door, he looked up indulgently, only to say, "Let's just hope he can play bridge," then continued on, brow furrowed. We then went looking for our mother, who was in her greenhouse wielding a small brush, pollinating. She looked up and smiled as we entered.

"My wards."

"Mother!" I said excitedly. "A rabbit has moved in next door."

"I think he is more a hare," said my sister.

"In the abandoned hutch by the forest?" my mother asked, not really paying attention.

"No! No! In the house next door! And it's not just a rabbit," I stammered.

"Hare," corrected my sister.

"Hare!" I shouted. "With a circus!"

"And a hearse!" added my sister.

"Oh," mother said, putting down her brush distractedly. She pushed a loose hair back behind her ear. "A hare?" she asked then, quite seriously, "Was he wearing white driving gloves?"

"Yes!" we shouted in unison.

"But how did you know?" my sister asked. "Did you see him arrive too?"

"No, no." she said. "I fear …well, not fear… I believe that I know him. He is a photographer. I knew him years ago. Oh dear," and patting our heads as she passed, she left the room.

We rushed back outside to watch the procession. When we got to the gate, there was a fog of dust from all the trucks. We dared not enter the grounds but stood watching and taking an imaginary inventory.

"The elephants must be in there," my sister said pointing.

"But he is not a circus leader, he's a photographer."

"Photographers need elephants just as much as circus people do," she countered. "Still, maybe not an elephant. Perhaps a hippo, like Mr. Barnum."

"I can see his car by the front and the door is open, so he must be inside," I ventured.

"How odd to have a hare as a neighbour. I should think that he is very friendly; at least now that it is no longer March. I do hope he is friendly."

"Do you think he burrows with his nice clean suit on?" I asked.

"Hares don't burrow, silly, though you can ask," she said laughing.

"Ask what?" and suddenly, coming around the other side of the gateposts was our new neighbour, smiling.

He was taller up close and somewhat intimidating in his immaculate suit with his ears erect. He reached out a hand. "You can call me Mr. H," he said. "And to whom do I have the honour of speaking?"

"My name is William and this is my sister," I said nervously, shaking his hand. He bent down and taking my sister's hand, kissed it with gorgeous civility. "Delighted," he said and smiled.

"We thought you were a circus," said my sister boldly.

"Well today I am somewhat," he replied.

"Do you have an elephant?" she continued.

Mr. H clapped and laughed. "I wish I did. Excellent transportation. Civil. Have you ridden on one?"

My sister and I looked upon him with awe. "Have you?" I asked.

"I traveled in India for a time. I came to know elephants. Civil chaps really. Just big, like whales…" his thoughts trailed off and he focused his attention on the spires of our house. "Is that your house there? Are we neighbours then?"

"Yes, that's our house," I said. "We have never seen anyone live here though. We think it is haunted!"

"Haunted! How delightful." He smiled, his whiskers bristling like plucked wires. "When you have ghosts, you have everything."

My sister and I looked at each other and fell instantly in love with our new neighbour.

"Do you live with your parents or are you wards of the state?" continued Mr. H. "Barons? Baronesses? Stranded? Orphaned? Parents lost, raised by sadistic nannies and cheeky butler types?"

"Oh no," my sister cried. "We live with our mother and father. He is an inventor and hopes that you can play bridge."

"Ah, cards. Practical man, and your mother?"

"She grows flowers," said my sister.

"She's a botanist and keeps bees," I added.

"There is an apiary then? How delightful again. I live for the drowsy summer bumble of..." and then he stopped. "Your mother is a botanist and your father an inventor?" he asked quite seriously.

"Yes, and he works in the city sometimes," my sister said proudly.

Mr. H drifted slightly then looked down at us and said, "Where are my manners? I have a lovely wicker picnic hamper in the car. The tea, I fear, may be cold and the lemonade warm, however we may find something to your liking."

Fueled by the desire to stay with our new friend and to see inside the house that had haunted our joint imaginations, we shouted, "Yes please!"

"Wonderful!" he replied clapping his gloved hands and bowing in a very theatrical way.

We began to walk along the side of the drive as trucks rumbled by. Over the years the grass had turned mostly to weed but it looked lush and green while the trees, heavy with spring blooms, were bent over, their branches almost touching the ground. Perennials pushed their heads through the earth to be met by a carpet of bluebells tentatively fingering out from the forest.

"We live on the other side of the hedgerow," my sister said. "Ah yes, so you do," replied Mr. H. It was difficult to keep up with his pace, his great long legs taking enormous strides.

"There is an old wall, too," I said. "In most places it is quite high and whoever lived here had broken glass stuck into the top all along the wall."

"It's scary," said my sister.

"Indeed," answered Mr. H. "Yet your parents must know who owned this house before. I was told it was a magician. Actually, I was led to believe it still is a magician who is the owner. They mentioned someone of a reclusive nature at the rental office. I had to make out a year's worth of cheques to someone whose name is prefaced with 'The Great...' Now isn't that mysterious?" he said, cocking an eye.

"Yes, though you and the elephants..." giggled my sister.

"Ah yes, my elephants and I, we are a mysterious bunch," said Mr. H and he waved his hands in front of our faces.

As we got closer to the house he pointed to the car and said, "The hamper is in the boot." He produced a key and waking over to his car, unlocked the trunk. From inside came the faintest scent of lavender, rosemary and earth. "My herbal garden. I never travel without it. For spells..." he said splaying his hands and affecting a dramatically ghoulish voice, "...and portents and pasta sauce!" He laughed. "Mind the pots," he said as he pulled out the hamper. "Come inside and I will pour the refreshments. Perhaps we can explore this house together? Oh, but wait, again, my manners. Are you expected home? Am I monopolizing you and spoiling your parent's tea? Perhaps you have lessons? Fencing? Sword dancing? Algebra?"

"Today is Saturday," my sister said, "and everybody knows this is 'when-we-stay-away-from-our-parents until-after-tea' day."

"Ah, well then," replied Mr. H. "Shall we be like Burton and explore? I sense the Nile does not begin or end here but as this is the house of a magician, perhaps other mysteries will envelope us. Shall we begin? But first," he said again, opening the hamper which he had placed on the pediment rounding the front stairs, "tea or lemonade?"

Upon entering the house we were instantly swallowed up by darkness and a close musty smell. Mr. H drew back an enormous drapery that covered the doorway and suddenly the great hall came into view. It was huge and much more formal than our practical foyer. Across the room, a stairwell arched out from the bottom then divided halfway up to different regions of the second story. Above the landing was an immense stained glass window. Though caked with dust inside and dirt outside, the basic design was still visible. It seemed to be a mustached man in a black suit, pulling a rabbit out of a top hat. He was posed rather pompously in a scene more suited to the Virgin Mary, surrounded by a lush forest of roses and tulips, trees and shrubbery, all rendered with a distinctly religious tone. "There really is no accounting for taste," sighed Mr. H as he turned to us. The floor was a dark and light marqueterie, covered entirely with a film of white dust except for the thin trail made by the movers.

"Do you mind if we proceed up to the top?" asked Mr. H. "I rented this house for a specific reason and have only seen it with words and a few amateur photographs." We nodded. "Northward then," he exclaimed, thrusting his arm forward and mounting the steps quite energetically. We followed excitedly. "I am a photographer. I was told the top floor of this house is made entirely of glass. A studio with as much natural light as nature can muster."

"It must be as hot as the greenhouse in the summer," I said.

"Let us hope proper ventilation did not escape the architect," he countered.

Up we went, explorers all. Each floor seemed to twist and turn illogically. Some rooms we passed look as though they had just recently been lived in while others were completely bare. Some furniture sat safely under yellowing sheets while other bits were openly moldering. Some windows were shuttered, others broken and through some you could see the sea. In the more secluded reaches, there was only the sound of our footsteps on the carpet but in other strangely resonant passages, we could hear the movers below quite clearly.

"I imagine it will take some time to sort out this house although I am not really sure I want to solve its mystery," said Mr. H. "The house has five stories though I suspect many more stories to tell. Perhaps we are all Pandoras and this house is our box?" He sighed. His voice had a deliberate inflection, a studied accent and though his tone was odd it had a lulling, soothing quality. On the fourth floor we turned and began ascending a darkened stairway. It grew quite warm at the top of the stairs and had a faint, acrid odor. "Ah," he said. Though we could not see in the darkness, we heard him fiddling with the rusted bolts of the door. My sister whispered, "How can he see what he is doing?"

"Why, look at my big pupils," he said turning, "and think of all the carrots I eat. Have you ever…"

"…seen a rabbit wearing glasses," my sister finished gleefully.

"Precisely," answered Mr. H as he flung open the door. "Oh," said Mr. H in awe. It was a marvelous room, all floor-to-ceiling glass with ornate pulleys hanging down from above. We were above the trees and you could see for miles — the sea, the forest and over to one side, the top of our house. I heard him say quietly, "I could ask for nothing better." He grasped the pulleys with his gloved hands, pulling and opening random panes of glass. "Wonderful!" he exclaimed. At the far end was a door to another room and a smallish, black pot-bellied stove. "Well. We certainly did not find the source of the Nile, but I do believe… I do believe we have found a large part of my future happiness. I wonder if there is any tea left?"

A few years later my parents were hosting a party. My sister and I were as drunk as everyone else and we slid through the house, crouching behind draperies or behind cabinets, listening to the stories of our parent's inebriated guests. We found Father in the dining room, sitting at the table with two men from his business in town and a whole host of spiritualists from the Society to which he belonged. He was clearly delighting in the utter

bafflement of his two colleagues as toasts were being made and drunk to 'The Cabinet'. We ventured
on, winding through the house, wondering where our
mother was. In room after room we found all manner
of partygoers but no sign of the hostess herself. Looking
outside, we saw lights on in her greenhouse office and
decided to surprise her. The door was slightly ajar and
we could hear voices within. We crept closer and tucked
ourselves behind a thicket of flowering shrubbery nearby, being careful to stay out of the door's line of vision.
Huddling close to each other we listened, exchanging
looks of surprise when we realized Mother was with Mr.
H, who seemed to be doing most of the talking. At the
time, it scandalized us completely and led to many late
night conversations between my sister and me — just to
try and make sense of what we'd heard that night. But in
later years, especially after our parents were lost, it helped
us to understand our mother much better, to see her as a
person, not just as our mother. And certainly it explained
a lot about Mr. H.

Chapter 12

MY SISTER AND I were buried in a huge feather bed in the attic of Mrs. Z's house. I was lying in the safe warmth of the blankets after being awakened early by the birds, watching as a tail moved around the bed — the orange cat Balthazar waiting impatiently for his daybed to be vacated. The walls slanted to a middle point, low shelves which ran the full length of the room were stuffed with books and bottles, and light streamed in from the round window above. On the far wall there was a huge carved chest of drawers, the window above it mirroring the one above our bed. Indian carpets lay haphazardly on the dark wooden floors and a well-positioned grate allowed the heat from the kitchen to waft up into the chilled room. My sister lay with her back to me, her finger in her mouth, her hair running out like someone had upended an ink pot over the bedclothes. When I finally slid out of bed, she murmured slightly and turned. I pressed my pillow towards her, which she wrapped herself around, and tucked the blankets under her. Balthazar jumped up on the bed with a grunt and a cackling meow, the beginnings of his daylong diatribe against disruption. The room smelled of pinecones and stove fires and sleep.

I made my way downstairs to the kitchen. The back door was open. "Goodness, you children do sleep in," said Mrs. Z from the garden. "I am quite envious. If Esme had her way we would never sleep. I do hope she didn't wake you?" Her daughter Esme could be seen nestled in the grass, her tiny hands reaching for a butterfly that flitted just above her. Mrs. Z reached over, "Yes, you are a precious one."

"We were up so late last night," I said standing at the door, rubbing my eyes. "We never stay up that late at home."

She was on her knees in ancient coveralls, unwrapping burlap from the bases of the trees that grew in the backyard. "Well then," grinned Mrs. Z, "you'll have to tell your parents what a bad influence I am on you." Across the luscious green of the lawn lay long strands of just-unwrapped fabric, looking as if a parade of summer snakes had recently discarded their skins as they slithered past.

"These trees have been so overworked they positively cannot breathe," she said. Esme, her hands waving, gurgled. "Yes precious, these trees were strangled with love. Oh, I could just strangle you." She caught my eye. "I was speaking metaphorically, though with *you* young man…" and she lunged at me, attempting to pull me down onto the grass. I squealed and fell, "…you may be the exception, my serious William…and your sister. The pair of you!" I was squirming with delight under the weight of her, twisting myself into knots in my oversized pajamas.

"I say," shouted my sister from the doorway. "Have you both gone off your heads? Mrs. Z, are you attempting to do my brother in? I do so hope as he is quite beastly."

"I was attempting, yes. Perhaps you could come and help me," she giggled.

Mrs. Z had come into our village the previous year. Her past was something of a mystery though she was not in any way mysterious. She always answered questions honestly.

"Whose baby?"

"Why, my own."

She arrived with very little — a cello, a small black cardboard suitcase, a steamer trunk (which contained a writing desk and library that folded within itself), an empty birdcage and her baby Esme in a knitting basket. Esme had red hair and looked nothing of Mrs. Z.

"I found her," was the answer she would generally give. "No, there is no Mr. Z."

Tall and dark, her skin was quite pale and had a constellation of freckles that spread out from her thin and pointed nose. She was all points — her elbows, her shoulders, her knees, her ears. She had gloriously crinkled black hair, which she wore on most occasions in pigtails, and languid brown eyes that dwelled behind black glasses. She spoke with a slight accent, clearly but quietly as if she feared being overheard, and she was always watchful, her eyes darting to Esme, to the conversation, the fire in the grate, a passing stranger, the shadow cast by a bird. Her long, elegant hands always placed flat on the table.

She was a writer and told us that she came from Canada. "The edge of the country where the rocks soar up and the sea is never calm," she said. "If you stand still long enough you can see it breathing and sometimes the water, black with life, can rise up and take you whole and never give you back. We painted our houses white and when the fog rolled in we were lost for days." She was also a clairvoyant. She read cards but was hesitant. "I will not answer questions and I can only see what is in front of me," she would say, shuffling.

She had written a book. "A tiny book of short stories from things my relatives had told me," she said. "Some were fisherman but most were just uneducated and drunk. However, when they looked out to the horizon, they saw so much more than I ever did. I was so worried when my book came out that someone would ask questions I could not answer, as honestly, I knew so little. I moved away the day my first royalty cheque came. It was so small but it was enough to take me to where I thought I should go. I felt that with that tiny book I had exhausted all the experience that I had, so I thought I'd better move and cast some sort of net to gather more. I didn't write a single word for another year; maybe it was more than a year. I moved to the city. I met this man while working in a bookstore...isn't that funny? Getting a job in a bookstore to look for experience for another book. He was looking for a book about *sound*, which I thought was equally as funny — reading about something you hear. He told me he provided sound effects for radio melodramas, and for the next two years I got paid twenty dollars a scream. My god, my poor neighbours," and she laughed. She also hinted vaguely at a magician she once knew who taught her the cards and how to focus her mind, "The right side of the brain is where we talk to ghosts."

Mrs. Z said that she had come to our village to write. She didn't feel, despite her time in the city, that she had gained anything but a few sweaters — and Esme — and now felt that she would rather write about someone else as that was what she did best anyway. When the Innkeeper told my parents of the village's newest inhabitant, they instantly sent an invitation to supper. My mother sent a small card and just underneath her formalities my father had scribbled in his purple ink, "and bridge?" From that first evening she became part of what my mother called "the close set." Mr. H had started dropping by for tea once or twice a week and there was Mr. P of course.

A couple of months after their first meeting, my father found a house for Mrs. Z across from the vicarage. It was a lovely old thatched cottage that leaned to one side, with a high stone wall covered almost entirely in holly, its red berries like pinpricks of blood. Rising above the wall were trees of all sorts, fastidiously pruned and fussed with. My father told Mrs. Z that although the rent on the house was cheap, it did come with addendum. "It seems the owner, some daft General or some such thing, will only let to someone who will tend to his trees. He has moved to Java for his health, though that does seem rather odd. The renter must send a bushel full of plums in plum season, apples in apple season etc. to him in Java. If all is met with his approval, the lease gets renewed until the next season bears fruit."

Mrs. Z fell instantly in love with the house and un-deterred said, "Sounds like a challenge." The following month, after letters were exchanged, she and her cello, suitcase, steamer trunk and birdcage — and Esme in her basket — moved in.

Mail would always find her. It turns out her tiny book had been quite successful and as her small mailbox would fill with cards and letters weekly, we assumed her publisher knew her address. "Only he," she said, "no one else. I would get nothing done if I had to answer the door all day. Besides, right now I have just enough cake for myself and Esme, and you and your sister — oh, and the lovely vicar who brings wine." Correspondence usu-ally remained unopened for weeks, gathering dust on the hall table. However, her reclusive ways changed out of necessity shortly thereafter. On the cork notice board outside the entrance to the vicarage she posted a small card with her name and address. It said: "Clairvoyant. Advice. Cello lessons. Tea." Her steamer truck, along with its books and writing desk, also yielded distilling devices and scales. "I've planted herbs in the garden, not in a witchy way, but I can certainly stir up a potion or two if pressed," she told us. She proved a great success with the well-healed villagers.

My parents were grateful for her presence and I believe she in turn was comforted by my family. She took to my sister and me a tad easier than to my parents and the close set. "They're so much smarter than I," she would say to me. "I feel the positive freak with my awful accent and lack of vocabulary." Mr. H would constantly send her flowers, which swam in bowls about the lovely still house and made it smell, she said laughing, "Like I've died."

I was entirely in love with her. One day during last summer, as we sat on the steps watching one of my parents' evening parties play out before us, I said, "I think you are simply the most beautiful lady in the world."

"Why, bless you, William" she said and kissed me. My first non-family kiss. She continued, "It's Mr. P though who fascinates me. I mean William, you are the one I love," she patted my leg, "but I believe it is he whom I will write my book about."

"Oh, he's ever so shy," I said.

"Still waters, William," patting my leg again, "still waters."

Mrs. Z rolled off of me, growing suddenly quiet after the insistent attack. "Have you written today?" I asked, trying desperately to seem the adult.

"Good Lord, are you my publisher?"

"Yes, well, Father said we should publish your next book ourselves."

"Oh William, it's okay. I know you just love me for my body." Unsure what she meant, I blushed.

"It is your mind that I love," I stammered. Mrs. Z laughed and pulled at the grass. "Well, you must be quite the young lad then, as when I was your age…no, wait… I've never been your age," she laughed again. A shadow came across us.

"Are you two in love or something?" asked my sister.

Chapter 13

EMILY WALKED UP the path towards Mr. H's house; the early autumn leaves crunching under her yellow boots. Above, a perfect arrow of birds headed towards the sea, black shapes against the slate gray sky. The air was chill and damp, and smelled of burning leaves and humus.

She was greeted at the door by Mr. Squirrel, Mr. H's assistant, who was neatening and attempting to tuck in his rumpled shirt. He wore a leather apron and wire-rimmed spectacles which he adjusted absentmindedly on a constant basis.

"Ah, Emily," he said out of breath. "Today is a work day. We are working."

"I brought you a flower," and she handed him a black iris which she had picked from the hothouse, "and I am to have tea with Mr. H. It's all been arranged."

"Well, thank you for the flower — how charming — and thank you also for the interruption. We've been going since morning and I am ever so exhausted. I am sorry I didn't know about your visit and impending tea or I would have popped into town for something better than jam cake."

"Oh, but I do love jam cake. However, it is somewhat of a secret," she pulled on his apron and whispered, "my being here at all."

"Ah, well then, a secret," said Mr. Squirrel, "this could explain my ignorance of the appointment." He adjusted his glasses and leaning down, winked and whispered, "I will be as silent as the grave. Mum is certainly the watchword," and he motioned her inside.

Little had altered since Mr. H's initial move, though he had replaced a few of the portraits. Any changes to the house, so as not to disturb its vibrations, had to be approved in writing by its mysterious owner. Drawings had to be sent to explain the proposed rearrangement of even the smallest bits of furniture and sometimes it would take months for approval to arrive before a couch could be moved closer to the fire or a carpet made more convenient to cover a chilly passage. At times Mr. H forgot what he had proposed, and upon receiving a telegram from Burma or Peru with the terse message, "Move the damned thing if you must," would be as much in the dark as the rest of the household as to what the *damned thing* was. He took to tying shipping labels on things he wanted moved — to remember — and carried a pocketful, and a pen, at all times. All around the house nearly every object had a tag containing a date, the proposed move and an arrow of its direction. Mr. H's letters were sent to the realtor who then forwarded them to a solicitor who then forwarded them onto the owner.

"He must know Mrs. Z's landlord," said Emily noting the tags. "Why do people seem to buy such lovely things and then never allow them to be sat upon or moved? It must be awfully boring for the couch to have to sit and see the same sights year in and year out. Poor Mr. Couch," she said consolingly, patting its overstuffed arm.

"It *is* queer," said Mr. Squirrel, shepherding her through the house.

Most of the house had been closed for the coming winter, it being too vast to heat, and with Mr. H's limited funds some rooms remained shuttered year round. Others, upon approval, had been stripped of their furniture for use in other rooms. Mr. H had replaced the hideous paintings that lined the walls up the main stairwell with a bizarre series of portraits of his relatives, all lying in state in their coffins. Emily always looked at them with a sort of glee and fascination. How odd they looked with their rabbit ears folded onto their sides, eyes shut as if sleeping, some with flowers, some wearing sleeping caps, looking so dignified in their last rest against the house's somber funereal walls.

Mr. Squirrel skittered up the stairs, now and then doubling back to answer a question or raising Emily up to see something she hadn't noticed before. He was a tall man and thus towered over Emily, and although his legs were long, he never took great strides but shuffled nervously when he walked. Emily clomped loudly, always enjoying the sound of her feet echoing though the house.

"We are all up on the roof. Although a gray sky, the light is nonetheless perfect, but we lose an F-stop every thirty minutes. I should say that very soon the light will be very much at rest and our working day will be very much over."

Emily loved Mr. H's rooftop studio. It seemed so exotic with its strange Turkish carpets and foreign smells — odd cigarettes that smelled of clove, and developing chemicals that smelled as if something had died — mixed with the salty sea air blowing through the opened vents and the strange damp earth smell from the plot of grass Mr. H was attempting to grow. That small bit of earth had not been mentioned to the owner and because of that, seemed every bit more enchanting to Emily.

Mr. Squirrel threw open the door, and both he and Emily entered the room. Mr. H was leaning against a table, a blue cloud emanating from his black cigarette, a cup of tea in his one hand. He was wearing a fez, his long rabbit ears down and back, and a red smoking jacket — his work clothes. Curtains suspended from the ceiling were pulled in various places to create a set. There were school desks and a number of pillows thrown haphazardly on the floor. Reclining on the pillows were the O sisters, with their dark hair and bottomless almond eyes, both wearing lavish loosely tied silk dressing gowns and black and white stripy stockings.

"Emily!" they shouted in unison and ran over to her. "Have you come to be in the pictures with us?" they cooed, curling her into them then twirling her around the studio. After recovering Emily brushed her coat, "I am here to have tea with Mr. H. It is a secret. Very hush-hush."

Mr. H exhaled and looked down at Emily. Behind

him, through the bubbling uneven glass, the sky was beginning to darken further. Mr. H stretched. "I'm tired," he said and looked to the O sisters. "We are all tired today." Stubbing out his cigarette, he continued, "So, Ambassador Emily, my young neighbour, you are here — some secret envoy from the Duke of Burgundy? Some intrigue and a little espionage before tea and the climb up the wooden hill to Bedfordshire?" He smiled and picked her up, grunting slightly. Emily put her arms out as if an angel, and when placed upon the table said, "You know why I am here — tea and…a jam roll."

The O sisters chimed, "jam roll!"

"Ah, jam roll," Mr. H laughed and turned to Emily, taking her hands and pirouetting her, chanting, "Jam roll and tea, diplomatic im-mun-i-ty. Now then, shall I order the tea…" he pulled a red velvet cord; somewhere in the house a bell rang, "…or business before pleasure?" He eyed Emily who put a finger to her lips and gestured towards the O sisters.

"My dear girl, they are family. Of course they are coming to William's birthday soiree…I am correct in this assumption?"

"We could dance a pantomime," the girls said in unison.

"Well," said Emily frowning, "there is a theme. I read it in a book that William is taking forever to write."

"Oh my, dress-up! I am very much liking this," said Mr. H, clapping his hands. Emily fixed him with a serious eye.

"This is serious," she said.

"I'm as serious as a…" Mr. H waved his hand,

"Whatever the metaphor is…"

"It's all very strange. But I thought we could all dress up and surprise him…or try to; he does always seem to know everything well in advance," Emily sighed. "He's been very beastly these past few weeks. Mrs. Z said he's been a mouse, but that doesn't seem right."

"I believe she meant *morose*, which very much does."

"Oh, well, yes," regaining her train of thought, "so perhaps we can cheer him a little, make him happy. He's making the house so sad."

"Dear girl," Mr. H took her in his arms and gave her a squeeze, pressing her face into the luscious luxury of his fur. He smelled of tobacco and bergamot. "This has been a melancholy coming to the end of summer, hasn't it? Here it is autumn just and the rooks have already packed and gone. It's just us left, our tiny lot." The O sisters came from behind the dressing screen, dressed now in matching black sailor dresses and the stripy tights from before. They were both quite pale from the day's work. Mr. H looked to them and said, "It is up to us to cheer the place. To light a lovely little fire." He waved his hands dramatically and picked Emily off the table and placed her on the ground.

A panel in the floor opened and the head of Mr. Squirrel popped up. "Tea things" he said and then produced a silver tea service which he slid across the floor. He disappeared only to pop up again with a silver teapot. "Tea" he said and slid that across the floor, then disappeared again. And then, lastly placing a plate of jam rolls on the floor and sliding them next to the tea, "Jam roll."

"Thank you, my dear Mr. Squirrel," Mr. H said,

"what a long day it has been. Take the rest of the day, the rest of the night. Do what you will. I will do the washing up."

"Thank you sir, thank you," said Mr. Squirrel, then descended back into the trap door, closing it behind him.

Mr. H smiled and paused, "Lovely man. Now tea! Sisters… come… tea… Emily, sit anywhere, we are very informal here." They busied themselves with the tea things, pouring, stirring, cutting the jam roll.

Then quite suddenly, as if someone dropped a purple cloth upon a lamp, the light changed to dark. A sigh came from the forest and there was, in that split second, the feeling that night had begun. A lone star popped into the sky like a pinprick.

Mr. H gazed out to sea. "We are so away from it all here. So spoiled. So lulled. It is just so lovely. I do hope I can spend all my days here… here with these wonderful people…" He walked over, kissing the O sisters on the top of their heads, sighing. "You can forget. I look across the sea and imagine the horrors, the absolute horrors that take place every day. Every Day. There is such a thin thread that binds us to sanity, and it's love. But we have to remember how delicate and fragile it is.' He sighed again, "Not here though. There is no horror here, our little port in the storm. God what a mess it is out there!" Mr. H punctuated. "Plagues and hunger! Prejudice and cannibalism! Governments! Popular music! Zippers! Wedgwood china! Automobiles! Gossip! Mean-spirited people! Horrible!" He stirred his tea. "Now, Emily, what *is* this book that our stuffy William is writing?"

Chapter 14

THE O SISTERS, Elsbeth and Harriet, lived in a lighthouse more than a mile to the east along the coastal road. The tower was out of service and slated to be torn down, but they lived there just the same, and nothing was ever said of the impending threat. It was a cozy cone of mismatched furniture and art from the artists they'd posed for, and the so-many suitors who came to woo them. I would find myself riding my bike there now and again as a sort of respite from the house and my family. They always welcomed me and as I grew, I became more and more fond of them, from infatuation to this realization that they, too, were an integral part of our community of misfits.

"We were Siamese twins," Elsbeth said.

Taking the Ouija board out of its box I gave her an incredulous look. "It's true, isn't it Harriet?!"

"It is," said Harriet, placing a bowl of cherries onto the floor beside me. "We were joined at the shoulder blades in our mother's womb. Cherry? As we were coming out, we were breach, and all the violence of being born tore us apart. That's why we're so close now, we shared nerve endings, they're near the surface." She pulled her top over her shoulder and turned. "We both have identical scars; Mummy used to say that it looked like we once had wings and had them removed."

We were on the main floor of the lighthouse, seven flights of spiraling staircase up. The room was, obviously, round and remarkably well lit to be only mid-way up the tower. The floors were all raw pine and worn to a shine. The walls were whitewashed brick. All the furniture was white wicker and covered in hundreds of pillows. Plants of every kind in pots and cups and champagne glasses were scattered about. A pet raccoon, Bertrand Russell, wandered and tittered and stole food off of plates. It was mid-winter and the chill sea wind whipped about the structure. We were warm and cozy inside. Harriet had made a fire in the stove and it crackled and popped and gave off the loveliest of scents. I scrunched my toes in my socks.

I met the O sisters through Mr. H, who used them almost constantly as his models, and the work he did with them — what I was allowed to see — was quite popular in the city. He would occasionally, through me, forward mail from ardent bankers and admirers of the kind of artistic photography that Mr. H specialized in.

"How long have I known you both?" I asked, lying back.

"Ages, let's not count, it's bad luck."

"But how long? Certainly since my sister…, since my parents."

"Don't you remember? As long as Mr. H. We've

been here longer, but we only met your family through Mr. H. We often saw your father and mother in town and they were always charming, but we had no excuse to introduce ourselves. The days were longer then. Now they come and go. We used to think in hours, didn't we?"

"Minutes," said Elsbeth.

"And then hours, days, now we're old, old, I lose whole weeks." Harriet moved the Ouija board on the carpet into a patch of sun.

I looked up squinting. "Why is it so sunny here?"

"Mirrors," they replied.

"I do hope we are successful today," Harriet said, pulling her legs crossed in front of her. "Ghosts, real ghosts only come out at dusk and dawn, when the light is changing from one world to the next. I don't think we have to worry about releasing any errant spirits this afternoon."

"No," Elsbeth said.

"Do we have a plan?" I asked. Bertrand Russell picked a cherry from the bowl and began washing it in my glass. "Bertrand," I shooed, "use your own bowl." He chittered at me, the kettle began to wheeze.

"Tea!" the sisters said.

Elsbeth jumped up and began preparing the tea things, twirling in the kitchen, "cucumber sandwiches....mm-mmm" Harriet lit incense, waving it about the room, humming and skipping slightly. "Princes, princes where are they, where are our princes to carry us both away?"

"Unable to tie their shoes," Elsbeth said pouring the water. "Save you, William. Oh, William, why are you so unavailable?"

"Elsbeth, you've known me since I was a child, it would be like incest."

"I wasn't proposing to sleep with you, I was just wanting to marry you. You could marry me and we could all move to the house; no, better, you and Emily move here, that house is far too haunted for your own good."

"And what about me?" questioned Harriet, stuffing incense sticks into the earth at the base of an aspidistra.

"Why you'd be here too, nothing would change, we would just have William and Emily about."

"You'd have to quit smoking," Harriet said sitting down again.

"William is used to it." She sighed then said wistfully, "But for Emily it would be worth it."

Chapter 15

THE HOUSE SMELLED of damp and ozone as we paraded inside. The storm broke and we all rushed inside in single file, laughing and slipping on the wet stone walk.

"Careful, everyone inside," I shouted, my voice filled with the first genuine happiness that I'd felt in ages. The rain thudded against the stone, turning it drop by drop from gray to black. First in was Mrs. Z in her bathing costume, still holding the lit lantern on the end of a stick. Mr. P held the door open, directing Mr. H, Emily, the O sisters and myself as we raised our hands to shield ourselves from the icy rain.

Mr. H approached me and put his arm around my shoulders. "Rain," he said. Emily seemed pleased, she had a great look of satisfaction on her face. She gestured for Mr. P to come over to her and he crouched down so she could whisper. "Ah," said Mr. P.

"It seems we...," Mr. P started, and then was interrupted by a crack of thunder; Emily squealed and the O sisters jumped. "We are to all to follow Emily into the attic, I believe she has a surprise for us up there." Emily looked at Mr. P. "Shhhh," she said.

"Oh, my, sorry, that was a surprise also, well, ahem, we are to follow Emily and trust her to bring us to safety from this dreadful storm, shall we then?" and he gestured to Emily, who purposefully stepped to the front and said in a ghostly voice, "Follow me."

"How delightful," said Mrs. Z, excited by the secret. I sensed however, that everyone save me was privy to this surprise. How well-timed the rain had been, I thought, and what an interesting parade we made, climbing the wooden stairs that creaked under our weight. Mrs. Z's light swished back and forth and then out of sight as she turned the corner. The pictures on the wall moved and quivered. The damp cold of the house followed us as if we were descending down to the cellar and not rising, stair by stair, up to the attic.

We all walked along the hall — something everyone in this party had done countless times — yet tonight it seemed queer, formal, as if we were on a guided ghost tour led by an over-enthusiastic eight-year-old. Emily turned to us and shushed. We, en masse, held our breath. She took out a candle and said, "Mr. P?" Mr. P reached into his pocket and produced a box of matches. "My dear," he said as he struck the wooden match against the box, cupped his hand and expertly lit her candle. Emily's tiny face was suddenly visible in its pool of yellow light, her black hair blending into the darkness of the hall. I felt a sudden spasm, a thin puncture of sadness thinking of my sister, but I pushed it away.

"There is magic about," said Emily, waving the candle with the whole of her arm so it nearly guttered out.

"Today the veil between the living and the dead is thin; it is All Souls' Eve and it is William's birthday,"

"Here, here," Mr. H clapped and there was general jostling from everyone else. Another clap of thunder and a crick-crack of lightening suddenly illuminated the hall and its contents. The storm was directly above our heads; the cold air rushing in from the sea, catching up to the stranded late fall warmth that had been hiding in the forest.

Emily continued, moving the candle to light the entrance of the attic. "Through this door is another world," she then brought it back to her face, "by stepping through it, everything changes. Everything we think is real will vanish."

I felt a slight tingling, as if someone was lightly tickling me. I turned to see that as the fur on his neck was raised, Mr. P must have been sensing it also. He looked to me and nodded very slightly.

"All ye who agree to walk through this secret door must agree to leave everything behind. This is a warning." Emily intoned.

"Goodness," the O sisters said in unison.

"Yes, quite" said Mr. H.

"Emily, I have goosebumps" said Mrs. Z, brushing her arms for warmth. On cue, the huge hall clock chimed eleven.

Emily then whispered, "The moment has come." She knocked a curious knock on the attic door. The same curious knock echoed back from within. "Follow me," she hushed and the candle guttered and went out. We all exclaimed as one. I could hear Emily struggling with the handle of the door, there were footsteps on the other side leading up to it, a sudden clack, and then the door swung in.

I was not prepared for what I saw. Hundreds of candles burned in candelabras, on plates and on the floor; so many that they generated a palatable perfumed heat that hit us, almost knocking us back after the chill of the hall. Lit pumpkins, cut with faces, were scattered creating a path. The entire attic had been done up as if it were the inside of a sultan's tent with a rich blue and white stripped fabric fixed to the centre of the ceiling. It billowed out and was attached half way down the walls, and then was left to drape down to the floor. Persian carpets were spread haphazardly upon which colourful pillows were scattered about. Garden furniture was placed here and there, mixed with plants in pots and birdcages with twittering finches. Picnic lunches had been set up, tea and sandwiches, wine, glasses and cutlery. At the far end a stage had been set up with gauzy drawstring curtains and lights. I was overwhelmed.

"Emily, all of you, this is beautiful. What a magical birthday..."

"William, shush," said Emily and walked into the middle of the room. We all followed her in; I sensed everyone feeling the same as I, that we had entered another world. If it weren't for the thudding of the rain on the roof, we could have been anywhere, some magical time, in the desert in a sultan's tent, the midnight sky indigo with a splash of creamy stars.

"Please sit where you'd like; there is cake and tea," Emily said, continuing in her circus barker voice. She clapped her tiny hands and the O sisters ran behind the stage curtains. We all found pillows and lowered ourselves to the floor.

Emily walked to the front of the stage and said "Ladies and Gentlemen, thank you for coming with me this far. I give you now a window into the beyond," and she clapped her hands again. Behind the curtains there was the scratching swish of a Victrola needle, then the unmistakable sound of Enrico Caruso, far off, singing *Mi Par D'Udir Ancor*. The curtains then magically opened and there was the most beautiful stage set of the sea. Shimmering purple cloth vibrated gently like waves, helped by a small electrical fan off to the side. The backdrop was painted with a cluster of stars and a moon; in the centre, a golden powder like moonbeams rained down. To the music the O sisters arose, scantily clad in translucent white gowns that floated about them like mist. Everyone clapped, though it felt odd to be doing so. Was this a dream? The O sisters twirled out of the waves — I have never seen movements so delicate; their hands, their arms, so graceful and lovely, they seemed suspended just off the ground by wires, lightly touching the scuff on the carpet and then back into the air. I fell in love, in that moment, with them. I felt I could write a novel just by knowing them. I felt so warm and loved, together with my closest friends in this magical setting. Mrs. Z holding her knees to her chest; Mr. P a little uncomfortable on the floor; Mr. H relaxed, indulged and smiling. The O sisters' moving about the room, stirring the candles flames, their delicate perfume. I uncorked a bottle of wine and filled the glass beside Mrs. Z. She turned to me, entranced with the dance, and smiled. The O sisters finished and stood in the centre of the stage. We all clapped. Mr. H shouted 'Bravo! Bravo!' They bowed, gracefully and then floated off behind the stage. The curtains came down.

"Well, William," said Mr. P leaning over as I filled his glass, "that is not something one sees every day. Such graceful sea nymphs. Lovely. And I sense there is more to come. Emily has really outdone herself. She told us we weren't allowed to bring gifts, but I have something for you. A little something that was left in my house once." He reached into his pocket and pulled out a small, delicate box. "That time your sister stayed with me, she left this behind and I've kept it always as it reminded me of her. When she was in my house, and Mr. Flowers agrees with me, she lit it from within. I miss her every day." He handed me the box. I felt a wave of nausea, more sadness than I could control mixed with incredible longing. "I so hope you don't think it out of place. It may seem a little morbid, but I see it more as a totem, a protective charm."

I took the box from him; it was light, hardly anything. It had at one time been covered in a red velvet, but that had been bleached and worn and was now a texture more than anything; the edges were worn right down to the wood of the box. I opened it. Lying in a black velvet sea was a blue beaded hair barrette. I breathed in. I felt as if I had been handed a holy relic. It spoke of her. It glowed of her. This tiny object, so mundane and everyday, once touched her. It was so commonplace and yet so, oh so profoundly important. I fingered it slightly and began to cry.

"Oh William, it was to make you happy. We never got to say goodbye to her, and she left us so little. I thought it touching. It is blue and I opened it to the moon every night. I would open the box and place it by the window. Mrs. Z told me to do it. Apparently now it will protect you, and keep you from harm. Our little Emily is the living memory of her and she, too, is here, I think, to protect us."

"Mr. P, I'm not sure what to say." I stuttered a little, so overcome, "Thank you."

"It is nothing, and everything."

Emily came out in front of the curtain. The wine was taking its effect on me and I glowed. Mrs. Z re-filled her glass. "Ladies and Gentleman," Emily said as she waved her arms dramatically, "For your enjoyment, recently returned from America with the secrets of the beyond…" Mrs. Z sat up. Emily wound the Victrola up again, Vaughan Williams. Emily clapped and the O sisters, still in costume, ran out and began blowing out most of the candles in the room and we were suddenly in half darkness, what little light there was caught the sparkles of the translucent curtain, setting them off like stars.

Emily then clapped again and said, "I give you… Esme and her trusted gentleman assistant." The curtains opened. There was a huge tank made of glass and filled with water in the centre of the stage. This time the set was a midnight forest, all blues and moonlight. The trees were all painted in back silhouette. It was eerie to see. A black bird, a rook, alighted on a branch. A naked white arm came out from behind one of the trees. The rook cocked its head to one side, shuffled its feet then flew over to land on the arm. Esme stepped out from behind the tree and said, "I have before me three sets of locks and a blindfold."

"Is this the best birthday ever William?" Emily asked.

"Yes, I think it is."

"It's just like the book you're writing."

"It is, isn't it. And what about yours, what about your book about all the *other* people in this house?"

"Oh William, I finished that ages ago."

Isabelle and Charlotte

ISABELLE SLEEPS WITH seven mattresses piled high on her bedroom floor. She climbs up on a chair to get on top. She had dragged all her furniture out into the hall and painted her walls the colour of eggplant, spotting the hardwood floor. She pulled her dresser back in and painted it black.

On Tuesday, Isabelle walks to school. It is autumn and the dead leaves crunch under her boots. The early morning air is so clean and cool; she pulls it into her lungs and breathes out a dragon's breath of steam. She hums.

At lunch, the only shop that carries the CDs she likes has something she has never seen or heard before and she buys it, counting out the exact change onto the counter. The clerk, who knows Isabelle but only from seeing her at the store, slips the jewel case into a purple bag with a gold crown printed on it and hands it to her; Isabelle's hands are so small, like a doll's — the clerk is always moved by this.

Isabelle decides to skip the rest of the afternoon — it is only math; she already knows it, she can hum Pi. She walks back to her family's apartment. Her mother is at work. Her father is dead. Isabelle barely remembers him. The lobby is empty; it smells of yellow disinfectant. The plastic palm trees seem alive in the gloom of the afternoon light. She stares at the elevator floor numbers set in silver as they descend to one, then steps inside.

She climbs up onto the bed. Her room is warm. She has made cinnamon toast — brown sugar, cinnamon and margarine to make it stick. She eats and watches as the crumbs flitter down like burnt snow onto her sheets. She brushes them away. The electric alarm clock actually ticks. Street sounds float up from seventeen floors below. She puts on the CD and closes her eyes. Music sounds better when you are not supposed to be listening to it.

Isabelle writes an email to a boy who's in love with her. She attaches a poem she wrote. She doesn't love him back but she's too nice to tell him (or just lazy). She writes automatically. Words are easy for Isabelle.

Emily is Isabelle's mother. Emily makes dinner listening to the music coming from her daughter's room. It is always loud yet no one around them seems to complain. There is a thud; Isabelle has dropped a book to the floor. Dinner tonight is simple — three tins, two pots, two dishes, two glasses, two forks, twenty silent minutes to make, ten silent minutes to eat.

"School?"

"Same."

"Life?"

"Same."

Isabelle helps Emily with the dishes then goes to her room. The music comes back on. Emily is tired. She works in an office where she has little to do, which exhausts her. She emails herself travel plans; she looks up itineraries, calculates prices, concocts schemes, which occasionally she sends to Isabelle. Isabelle never answers her mother's emails. Emily sits on a couch that faces the sliding doors, the balcony, the south, the city and the lake. Autumnal lightening ripples like sweater static over the lake. No sound, just a flash of green light over the water. Emily falls asleep and dreams of the sea.

On Wednesday, Isabelle walks to school. It is a perfect autumn day and the dried leaves crunch under her feet. She cannot hear them as she has her earphones on. She breathes in the cool air.

The houses pass by.

School today is the same, nothing learned and nothing gained. Art first thing. A self-portrait which she hates; she's made her eyes blue solids and the teacher has to show the entire class. Isabelle smiles and thanks her. Isabelle has always been good at art. The boy who is in love with her is in this class and he slips a note to her via Sarah. It's covered in little drawings of hearts. This irritates her, both the hearts and bringing Sarah into this, but she makes eye contact. She smiles and slips it into her journal, hoping he thinks that she'll read it later. In fact, it nauseates her thinking about it.

At lunch, Isabelle sits with her friend Charlotte. They have known each other since Grade 9. It's now Grade 10. Charlotte hands Isabelle half of a sandwich as Isabelle forgot hers. Isabelle sees her lunch bag sitting in a square of sunshine on the table in the silent kitchen. Isabelle feels sick/sad thinking about her mother coming home from work and seeing it. She will try and get home first and throw it away. Isabelle eats the half sandwich and asks Charlotte about the boy who's in love with her. They plot a way to make him go away.

After lunch, it's English. Isabelle gets tired half way through as no one has read the book save her, so most of the class is spent listening to the frustrations of the teacher. Isabelle opens her notebook and writes a poem. She knows she's not very good at poetry, but who is? She writes a poem about the time she and her mother went to the sea. She turns the page and the note from the boy is there. She feels sick but opens it and reads. He spelled *devoted* wrong. She suddenly feels so sorry for him and decides she won't let him know how she feels for a while, just a while. Maybe he'll get bored, maybe he'll move away, it would be easier.

She looks out the window and sees Charlotte in her gym clothes running after a ball with her field hockey stick. The teacher blows a whistle and they all suddenly stop in time. Charlotte waits. Isabelle wonders what Charlotte is thinking. The teacher blows the whistle and they all move again frantically about the sparse, brown field. Isabelle shakes her head to wake herself and tries to focus her eyes on the blackboard. The teacher has written "For next week…" Everyone is writing it down.

Two nights a week Isabelle serves food to seniors. She hates it because she knows one day someone like her will be serving her food and hating it. The rooms always smell of candy and urine and she swears she smells like that all the way home.

She moves silently towards her apartment building, walking with deliberate steps, listening to the houses. Overhead, the bare tree branches reach into the centre of the street — indigo sky, then black, then indigo, then black. There are a few brave stars. Tonight for the first time this year she feels cold.

Her mother is home when Isabelle gets there. Her lunch is no longer on the table and nothing is said of it. In her room Emily has placed folded laundry by her bed, stacking it small to large, everything descending, article by article; underwear on top, folded into squares, down to the bed sheets. It depresses Isabelle. She picks up each section and places them in her painted black dresser.

Emily walks by Isabelle's room and reads the song lyric stuck to the outside of the door. Isabelle hears her out there, knowing she will not come in. Both stand still, listening. Then Emily walks away.

On Thursday, after school, Isabelle goes home with Charlotte. They are working on a school project, the very thought of which makes them both very tired. They sit on Charlotte's bed and listen to music. Charlotte's bedroom has stayed the same since she was five-and-a-half. Her mother works in the same office as Isabelle's. Her father is an architect. Charlotte changes the CD then lies back on the bed with Isabelle.

"When I was 10," Charlotte starts, "I was so sick my parents were told to prepare for the worst." Isabelle rolls over and looks at Charlotte; she notices a pimple forming, a red dot, just under her nose. "I got better but my parents never got over it."

At dinner Charlotte's father makes remarks that Isabelle doesn't understand. Not that they are over her head, they are just not funny. Charlotte's father laughs alone at his remarks. Isabelle thinks of Charlotte's father alone in a car, laughing to himself. She looks at Charlotte who doesn't seem to acknowledge her father at all as he laughs. Charlotte puts her hand over her mouth when she chews or talks.

When Isabelle gets home, her mother is sitting on the couch looking out the window holding a glass of wine. She often does this. The apartment smells of the dinner just eaten; a low cheese smell, which makes her feel ill. In the kitchen she takes down a glass (the one with yellow flowers, not the 'Souvenir of St. Thomas' one) and fills it full of water from the filter in the refrigerator. Tacked to the door is a picture of Isabelle when she was six, holding a fish. Isabelle has no memory of this picture being taken, this place, of catching a fish. She puts her finger on it and leaves a small smudge. Also on the fridge, held with a magnet, are an unfinished grocery list and a calendar with the days x'ed in red when her mother goes to yoga.

On Friday, Isabelle has trouble waking up. Emily grows impatient because if Isabelle is late, so is she. Isabelle moves about the kitchen weighted down with sleep. She is wearing a black T-shirt so long it goes below her knees. Emily stares at her daughter and wonders who this person is.

Isabelle walks to school listening to the CD she bought on Tuesday, using it as a soundtrack to the movie she is making in her head.

After school, she and Charlotte walk back to her apartment; Charlotte is staying over. In her backpack she has a bottle of wine that she took from her father's cellar. Though neither really drink she thought it would be cool to get drunk. Tonight they are going to write a novel. Charlotte talks about a trip she went on with her parents years ago. Isabelle watches Charlotte, her hands moving, directing the past. Charlotte is wearing her winter coat even though it's not that cold. A ski-lift tag has petrified onto the zipper pull. It's been there since last year, Isabelle thinks, yet she cannot remember Charlotte once saying that she had gone skiing.

It is now late, Emily says goodnight and asks if they need anything, and don't stay up too late, and goes off to bed. They drink the wine indifferently, not really feeling any sort of effect.

"My father said this tastes like chocolate," Charlotte says.

"What kind of chocolate does he eat?" answers Isabelle.

They light candles and listen to a CD quietly so as not to wake Emily. Their novel has not yet begun. It begins to rain. The girls sit and listen, soothed by the rhythm of the drops hitting the cement of the balcony. The room is suddenly filled with cool, fresh air.

Charlotte drifts a little, her eyes close. Isabelle notices that Charlotte smells of soap. They lay quietly for a long while, hours, until Charlotte gets up to pee.

Suddenly Isabelle is so unaccountably tired. Not just from the day, but of the night, of everything around her and in front of her. Even thinking about the future makes her feel tired. When Charlotte comes back, Isabelle goes to her drawer and takes out a length of black cord that she had bought for a sewing project she had never started. She takes the cord and wraps it around Charlotte's waist, loops it once, then wraps it around herself, tying it tightly around her own waist. Charlotte says nothing, does nothing, just watches Isabelle's face fixed on tying the knot. They flatten against each other when she pulls the string tight. Isabelle thinks of a song. She realizes that aside from her family, this is the most intimate she's ever been with anyone in her life. It excites her slightly.

The rain has increased; the patter of drops is constant on the balcony. The girls stare at each other without speaking. Isabelle moves them awkwardly towards the balcony door, like someone crossing ice, ill prepared, uncertain.

"Charlotte, I'm tired," Isabelle whispers.

Charlotte puts her head on Isabelle's shoulder, the seam of Isabelle's top pressing into her cheek. Isabelle presses her face into Charlotte's hair.

They move on to the balcony, the rain soaks them instantly. Isabelle thinks it must be late as so few lights are on. The CD in the bedroom has finished. The air smells of smoke from fireplaces.

"Isabelle…" Charlotte begins quietly.

Isabelle looks at Charlotte then closes her eyes. She puts her arms around Charlotte's waist and with one unbalanced motion pushes them up over the railing and into the night air.

Everything now is finished, what little there was is now gone. Isabelle watches Charlotte's beautiful face; they lock eyes, shadow to light to shadow to light. Time slows to nothing. Isabelle thinks of the first line for their novel, she begins to speak, but Charlotte has already gone.

The Book of Ghosts

I

THERE ARE TRICKS I can do by folding my hands as if signing to the deaf but when I sleep alone here beneath the roots, I wring my hands for warmth. There are others who come here too, though they are just passing. It's eerie how we do not talk but know each other. We sleep like a circus sideshow in tin trailers buried under the snow. I am the invisible man. I am ice.

II

ON NIGHTS WHEN she lets me into her world, when we climb the steps to the top of the house and look out over the cold midnight city, there is a sensation in my stomach like cat burglary. I have only been here when it's dark. She will not let me in until the house is asleep — this place where she lives, the lighted window of her seventh floor.

Bidding me past the threshold she turns and snaps on the lamp by her bed, placing her just-lit cigarette in an old Hilton ashtray. She has her own kitchen up here, a hot plate with a kettle that rocks as it boils. There is a small wooden bookcase containing schoolish books well-thumbed next to lurid horror novels and scattered notebooks. Beside it is an overflowing wastebasket of Kleenex.

A mass of dead flowers is placed in the mouth of a fireplace. Worn stuffed animals sit on a bed shaped like a sleigh. There are candles everywhere.

And movement.

A small toy car rolls back and forth on the fireplace

mantle, a box peers out from beneath the bed, then slides back under. A pair of scissors opens and closes continuously. She alludes to this constant movement with a gesture. "My ghosts," she says.

Sitting down she rummages through a shoebox. Absently she pulls out a photo of herself being held upside-down by a skinhead. Her face is weary, out of focus. She is 14, her hair in pigtails, black T-shirt, short skirt falling up, the holes in her torn tights like stars. The skinhead is shouting, angry, happy to be alive. He is wearing black jeans with suspenders, a black Polo shirt, DESTROY is tattooed on his bristled crown. People stand around, uninterested, in the preternatural light of the club marquee. She is so fucked up it hurts to look. On her arm is carved a phone number; the wounds are fresh and vicious. I glance now at the fragile arms coming out of her dress, brindled with scar tissue, the phone number faded to patchy white ghost shapes — a constellation of sorrow.

And the fresh scars on her arm (which we do not talk about).

Getting up she winds the key of a little tin Godzilla that spits sparks. Walking towards the door she sets it free.

She comes back with a spaghetti jar filled with water. Out of her desk drawer she pulls a Swiss army knife. A small pink plastic coffin with an erasure the shape of a skeleton falls to the floor.

"Thank you for the flowers."

She turns off the light.

There is a feeling of intense pleasure here, with the snow piling upon her angled windowpane. The sensation, though, is as much asphyxiation as it is intoxication, like being sealed slowly in a body bag.

Each time I come here I tell myself it will be my last. I hold her in my arms and feel her warmth as she folds into me, but her eyes focus on things that I cannot see. I am just another ghost to her. Yet I cannot shake this fascination with the tragedy she will not take me to.

She lights another cigarette.

She begins, "When I was 12 I had a friend." In the darkness I can just see the glowing tip of her cigarette. "She wasn't popular. She was tiny, smaller than me with jet-black hair that was cut in a harsh bob that didn't seem to hang right. Thinking about it now, the way her eyes were always set back, and how she walked, there was probably trouble at home — it's funny how you never think like that then. I made friends with her because she drew pictures in French class. Really cool spidery pictures of trees. She was so intense about everything. Everything mattered. It got scary sometimes how much she cared. One time it rained all week and I remember we were walking to school and the entire route was just covered in huge dew worms; big fat ones. She freaked. We were late for school because she had to place every one that she saw back on the grass by the sidewalk." She drags on her cigarette and brings her knees up to her chest.

III

ON NIGHTS WHEN she will not let me in, I sometimes go anyway, scaling the wall like an insect. I lie on her window peering in, watching her on the floor cutting shapes out of paper and sticking them in a book; cutting words from magazines; cutting herself. She knows I'm there. My silhouette falls on a carpet of scraps, my arms outstretched as if I've fallen from a great height. I lie there frozen, in the winter twilight, feeling her warmth a few feet away through the glass.

It's on nights such as this I reacquaint myself with hate and anger and cold, as in muted frustration I watch her destroy herself. Some nights I see a crown floating over her head as if she'd been sainted — my little saint. But there is no martyr's blood in her. What she spills is a conjurer's trick as she presses the blood from her vein, wincing as it trickles over her arm.

I watch her sleep. Curled and dreaming in the light of a candle, her face is relaxed though her body is tangled and tied in the sheets. I am struck by how small she seems — her delicate, crooked teeth, the fine hair on the nape of her neck. I can trace her veins and arteries, her muscles and bones. Hear her heart beating. I look at her homework on the desk and I long to climb inside and finish it for her — to sneak a poem in between the pages of her book. I feel ill and alone as I watch her. Suddenly the candle goes out and the paleness of her is gone.

Uninvited I pass alone through her house. I float upon the gentle scent of sleeping winter flowers through a labyrinth of pianos and books and clocks and silver curios from the East – her father is a collector. I creep up the stairs to where her family is, feeling the currents of their dreams wrap around me like water. They are asleep but I hear their voices. Hear her mother. Her father. Her. I float silently, just above the ground…

…and hear the slow ticking of the clock in the hall.

I enter a room made small by a piano. I run my fingers on its hard metallic strings, leaving the copper tarnished. The light from the dying fire makes the room move. Atop the mantle, resting against a small marble head, is a photo of her standing under a lilac tree. Looking so serious.

I hide it in my coat.

IV

MY FATHER HAS taken not to sleeping. He is standing at the window holding a deck of cards. He is getting smaller; he is getting grayer. His hands move idly, thumbs and forefingers moving the cards. I cross the snowy field to their house, which glows at the top of the hill. Behind it, the cove is frozen over with black ice framed by skeletal trees bent with wet snow. The wind carries me. He sees me coming and opens the door.

"You've come back...again."

"Is that all right?"

"Your mother's asleep, but you know that. Is everything all right."?

"I'm OK, lonely. And you, how is..."

"She doesn't really come out much — I do everything now. I've begun to notice things changing...colours...."

He beckons me in and deals out seven cards in a circle then puts the deck down. He turns the first card over — the hanged man. Turns it back. Scoops them up then passes them to me. I take the deck and lay out the foundation for a house of cards.

My father was a movie director in the 1950's. His films were quiet and filled with an uneasy sadness — they made people cry and long for lost loves or dream of things that they'd never have. His father, my grandfather, painted huge canvases of flowers. Each afternoon he would walk on the rocky shore where my grandmother died. One stormy day a wave rose and swept him out to sea.

My mother had been a circus conjurer, a performer of tricks. She would appear nude, wrapped only in a red cloth, which was then rolled out into the audience. The men would lean forward in anticipation but she would be gone. Her parents tried to commit her. She could read minds. She heard things. She has written fifteen novels that she keeps hidden in the bedroom closet, all of which start with the same sentence.

She met my father in a casino. They were both standing at the bar. He had seen her the previous day in a sideshow. He asked her for a trick. She offered to make his drink disappear. She pulled a silver dollar from his ear; he folded a napkin into a crane.

There is a tapping. My mother. She knows I'm here.

My father is writing a new screenplay. He writes in long hand with a fountain pen. His fingers are stained with green ink.

I add a second layer to the house.

"We miss you," he says, concentrating, taking a card and starting another room, "though these visits don't do any good. I'm always left with something unfinished. Why do you come back?"

"I need to see you. This is still the only home I have."

I float the house of cards off the table and turn it. Although he's used to this now, he still can't hide the wonder in his eyes. I shatter it; the air crackles. The cards fall into a pile, perfectly stacked in my father's hands.

V

THE ICE IS seven inches thick. Here under the water the moonlight shines through, creating a blue green floating frescoed ceiling. I can feel the current shift, see the ghosts of fish like leafy shadows. Surrounding me are the bags of spring kittens that my uncle threw away, mixed with buoys and anchors and sand from the Nile. I used to swim here in the summer until the muck moved into the cove from the septic tanks. The distant shore seems black and foreboding from below.

A small boy dressed in blue sits in a tree nearby. A huge raven circles the tree then lands beside him. He strokes its feathers and looks into its crimson eyes, not afraid. In its beak, it carries a golden ring and a bit of bone. It places them beside him, shifting from claw to claw, sniffing the air suspiciously. It caws and flutters its wings.

"Thank you," he says and places the ring and the bone in a tiny box his mother had made to collect bits of string.

The bird sits with him until the sky turns purple.

VI

THE DOCTOR RESEMBLES a marionette, a paper maché stick figure Satan. She is lying on the floor, blue. Her lips almost closed. Her eyes shut. He tosses his huge black coat aside, rubs his hands quickly to warm them and then leans into her, pushing on her body which bends under the pressure like a green branch. The doctor repeats the motion. Shouts, "Call 911."

She is dying.

Her mother, pushed away by the doctor, stands awkwardly to one side and keeps turning to me, as if she can see me; a face of fear. In the distance the sound of her father running.

She is dying.

Her body presses into the carpet, fading into the colour. There is movement in the room — frenzied — although the doctor, lost in the fight, cannot see. Candles light, drawers slam. Her head is back. Wisps of hair, like webs, frame her face. The artificially-pumped blood is moving to her brain. Her lips part.

Listen.

She walks over to where I'm standing. I tell her that this is not right. She stares at me. Says something about death. Looks away. I cannot hold her anymore.

In the shadows a man I had not noticed before steps forward. He looks much like the doctor, tall and in black. His face is sallow, his eyes sunken. He has a goatee. He moves over the body on the floor, his boot brushing the sleeve of the furious doctor. "This is wrong," the doctor shouts. The stranger comes to where we are standing, "Quaint, this," he says and with a flourish gives me his card. It is blank. She moves behind me. Strange dark clouds form above, in them faces, spiders.

The doctor is losing her; he knows it — we all do. He looks to the faces in the room. The stranger, struck by this, turns his back to us and moves to face the window. There are stains on his black coat. Outside, purple darkness. The hard snow reflects blue moonlight in a carpet of diamonds.

He waits.

On the floor she coughs, yet from behind me I feel her grip my coat. Feigning boredom, the stranger turns and pulls a book from a shelf and unfolds a pop-up house. He holds it up to his face and looks through it at me, an eye in each upstairs window. Yellow fingernails move into the pop-up garden. I feel her icy hands around my waist; she has worked up my shirt. It feels as if she is trying to climb inside of me.

The doctor continues now in a furry. The mother is crying, her husband holds her and looks away. A volley of ice pellets suddenly crashes against the windowpane.

Her grip loosens. I smell grass waving near the sea

baked by the summer sun. I smell lemons on a wooden table in a silent room. I turn and she is gone...

...replaced by screaming. The doctor. Her mother. Her. She vomits something black.

She is alive.

The stranger has his hands over his eyes. A small cat slinks into the room. It moves towards me and sniffs, then jumps effortlessly onto the bookshelf.

Silence.

Then breathing. A siren. Her mother sobs into her husband's arms. The doctor, disheveled, gently buttons her shirt. Covers her bruises.

I am helpless.

Receding into the shadows, we who do not belong, leave.

For Your Loss I Grieve

AT LAST MR. H could stop. He pressed himself against the crumbling trench wall and lit a cigarette. His fur was matted with mud and blood (some of it his). He had been going for 14 hours straight, carrying bodies on wood and fabric gurneys. Bodies that were once men, boys actually, who went over the wall filled with terror and little else and in seconds were reduced to nothing but bone shards and hair. He inhaled the acrid smoke of the cigarette into his lungs and tried not to think.

The view around him was desolate, a gray wasteland of skeletal trees where twisted bits of barbed wire rolled in the breeze. Somewhere a horse screamed in agony. Carrion circled silently, the only carefree movement. It had rained for two days, the dark black mud pulled like quicksand mixed with splintered bone and roots. There were six inches of fetid water in the trench, rainbowed with gasoline and swimming with feces and disease. Mr. H's legs and arms ached to the point he was numb.

He kept his ears tied back and down; even still, the blasting and screaming was so furious he was deafened. No birds sang, and if they did, he did not hear them. The stench, however, was palatable — a butcher's shop floor of offal and shit, mud and rot. The cigarette masked it, albeit briefly. The shelling had stopped. There were no charges, no shots from the artillery. The men around him sat on what they could — helmets, wooden shell boxes — and tried to rest. The silence grew. As he smoked he became aware of his heart beating, the low thud inside him, in his ears, upon his forehead. He stared at the faces wondering whom, with the next charge, he would end up carrying back in pieces.

He inhaled deeply and listened to his heart and thought of being clean. Suddenly a second heartbeat joined his — irregular, thudding. His own quickened, his whiskers and fur bristled; the second beat remained, deep, resonant, uneven. He closed his eyes and tried to listen. When he opened them, the men were running in the trench like rats trapped in a maze. He was confused and looked back. He blinked to clear his vision but there, in the centre of the trench was an enormous shadow, bouncing and skittering, a huge and monstrous thing. He blinked again and saw a mechanical ball covered in spikes and chains, out of control, careening through the trench, crushing men, smashing fortifications, bouncing this way and that. Bodies were impaled then smashed into the mud as it rolled on to the next. No one was safe; anyone who jumped up out of the way was instantly shot by snipers. The body of a young soldier that Mr. H had borrowed a cigarette from fell at his feet. In shock Mr. H stared. The boy looked at him and reached out, opening his mouth to say something, but instead of words blood and much of his insides came out all black and red and twisted. Mr. H leaned down and in a thud the metal ball came — close enough that he could smell the hot petrol stench, close enough that it tore his uniform and ripped his fur, close enough that as it passed it attached itself to the boy, bouncing away, crushing what was left of him into pulp.

"What manner of man thought up such a killing machine? Who could distance himself from this horrific death," thought Mr. H. Suddenly the earth rose up around him and blackness came and he remembered nothing else.

He awoke in sunshine — the yellow-white warmth of sun through a window. He looked down and saw his feet and a robe he did not recognize. He sat up quickly, remembering his duty, remembering the killing machine, then fell back down in an agony of pain.

"You are back with us, then?" said a voice, somewhere behind him. He found it difficult to open his eyes then realized there was a bandage over one.

"Where… where am I?" he asked.

"You are 20 miles from the front, in a hospital. You are safe," said the voice. There was then a pressure on his paw and he looked up to see a woman in a nurse's uniform checking his pulse and smiling at him. Her hair was pushed under her nurse's cap, her eyes were huge and brown; she was, Mr. H thought, perhaps the most beautiful woman he had ever seen. "This is a chateau, a winery, there are orchards all around us and a family living upstairs. I don't think I've ever been in a more beautiful house," she said.

Two beds over a man began to scream. She dropped Mr. H's arm and rushed off. The man was injected with morphine and stopped screaming. He had no legs and was heavily bandaged. In fact, everyone in the room seemed wounded beyond repair save for him. He tried to move his paws, his feet; yes everything was still there. He felt his chest; it was fine.

He was in a hospital. He was alive while everyone he knew was dead. He could still smell the trenches, still smell the mud, but there was a breeze coming through the window behind him carrying the scents of lilac and apple blossom. As the gusts lifted the curtains, patterns of lace shadowed themselves upon him through the sunlight.

"What happened to me?" he asked when the nurse returned.

"You were dug out of the mud unconscious. I don't really know all the details save that you were one of the few who survived. You were thrown away in the explosion and somehow got out of the way of the debris. That machine was filled with shards of glass and nails. Bolts. Screws. It was horrible. Men, half men, brought in, brought here to die really. There was nothing we could do. Glass was embedded into their faces. Razor blades. Razor blades. Who would do such a…who would make such a horrific machine?" She began to cry. Then caught herself.

"Who indeed?" said Mr. H, but he knew the answer. Us.

The nurse's name was Emilee and seemed to be his only nurse for she was there morning and night. He could feed himself so she attended mostly to his dressings and comfort. He was in a lot of pain and she injected him with morphine when it was really bad. When he could not sleep, which was most nights, she would sit in a chair, in the dark beside him, exhausted but alert in the silence. "You can hear the night," she said once.

Emilee spoke very little. She brushed out Mr. H's ears and tried to un-matt his fur where he was cut and the blood had caked thick. She had found him slippers and the robe, so when he was ready he would be able to move about freely.

He was awarded a medal and told he was being re-posted to a job away from the front, away from the killing. Now and then officers came by to check on him. He was well liked and there was great concern about his well-being. It embarrassed him, lying there amongst the dead and dying. He would roll over after each visit and fall asleep.

When he was able, Emilee took him out into the garden; the spring air was delicious and warm. He leaned heavily on her, unsure of his footing. He was so tall and she so small. He realized, though, that despite her size she was all muscle and strength. He watched her concern as she led him, hesitantly, onto the terrace then down onto the grass. He fell in love with her then for the second time. Right there. With her.

"There are peacocks in the orchard. There are so many, they move together like radiant clouds," she said. "There are children here today, moved here from the cities, sent away from the bombing to be safe. I cannot imagine what they are going through but children seem to always make the best of things."

"Yes," said Mr. H, pausing, feeling the sun pressing pleasantly down on him, "it's survival." He walked with her to be near the flowering apple trees, their blossoms bright in the unfiltered sunlight. Why here, he thought, only 20 miles away, is the light so different, so healthy and warm. He thought of the mud and the biting flies that came with it, caking itself to the soldiers' bodies as the sun baked them.

A group of children rushed past. They were all in short pants or dresses, looking so clean and well groomed; they probably just had their first warm bath in months. They were chasing the peacocks, which ran ahead, cackling and screeching into the trees. He was struck by the simplicity of that. How beautiful the trees looked in the sunlight, the children running and the impractical, exquisite and beautiful birds. He breathed in deeply, taking it all in, his lungs almost unsure what to do with such clean air, such decadent scent. He felt so weary and so calm.

"I…" he began when suddenly an intern in white ran towards them. "Stay back! Just stay back!" he screamed. Soldiers rushed forward from every direction. Suddenly there came a horrific blast, shaking the ground so violently he and Emilee fell.

Mr. H reached for Emilee but she pushed him away.

Then, the familiar silence.

Then, like gentle snow, apple petals and tiny bits of luminescent feather drifted down from the sky, all slaked with blood.

The Paris Apartment

THE LITTLE MAN from the floor above left another bottle of milk outside her door. She heard the bottle's glassy 'ping' as he placed it upon the tiled hallway floor, his feral footsteps echoing softly up the stairwell as he went on down. Crawling across the floor she reached up and unclasping the latch, pulled the door open. Looking dramatically out to the left then the right, she curled her fingers around the bottle and pulled it quickly back into the apartment. Camus the black cat rubbed up beside her and mewed. She frowned, "Kitty, you know I don't speak French."

Drawing her knees to her chest she leaned against the door, shutting it with a click. Peeling the paper stopper off the bottle, she sipped the cream that had risen to the top. "Mine," she purred to Camus, "all mine."

Through her greasy Parisian window a weak square of dawn light inched its way towards her. She thought to herself that however matter-of-fact that light was to the millions of Parisians sipping coffee from their bowls, it was still intoxicatingly exotic to her; it was light that had risen and yawned, warmed itself and daubed on eau de cologne as it crossed the early morning city, *rue* by *rue*. She touched the edge with her toe.

Her apartment was seven flights up a spiral seashell of stairs. There was a main living room with high, high windows and a long, dark hallway that opened on the left to the bathroom ("*le toilet*") and the kitchen ("*la cuisine*"), both with windows that looked out to the inner courtyard with its landscape of rippling laundry. On the right was the bedroom, which was the size of a small house and contained nothing but a tiny desk with seventeen notebooks stacked upon it (she had not been able to stop writing since she had arrived) and an Edwardian croquet set, which she set up one day by hammering the wickets into the hardwood. When she needed to think she would knock the balls about the room, making them bounce noisily, wood against wood, along the floor. The only decoration was a newspaper article about her sister in Milan that had been stuck to the wall with tape.

She got up, pulling her robe closer around her and headed towards the kitchen. Sliding in her stocking feet, she pretended she was skating and hummed a suitable skating song. The cat slunk around her, almost tripping her up.

The kitchen smelled of stale everything: the tea towel, the sink and whatever lived under it behind the green gingham curtain. A baguette from yesterday sat on the tiny counter with a knife and a wine-stained glass. A wine bottle sat empty in the sink. The floor was black-and-white tile that got dirtier the more she scrubbed and in the corner there was a cheese rind, curled like a giant's clipped toenail, that was currently Camus' favourite toy.

The cat mewed. "How could I forget you?" she said and opened the refrigerator, humming the refrigerator song. She pulled out an open tin of sardines.

"Kitty, I know you think I am incompetent but I promise today I will go out to the *supermarche* and buy you something that resembles cat food. *Nourriturment de chat pour M. Kitty*."

"Mew."

"You're welcome my little bear."

When Isador said "Emily," it sounded like "Imalee".

"But Imalee," said Isador, "why did you move here? Why did you come?" She deftly exhaled blue smoke over Emily's shoulder then twirled the ash of her cigarette in the ashtray into a point. Twirl, tap, tap. Twirl, tap, tap.

"Rouge, r-r-r-r-r-oug-g-g-g-e," Emily replied. Emily had drawn a moustache on her face with eye-liner before going out. She had only known Isador for a month, but Emily loved her because although Isador spent her entire waking life asking questions, she would never think to ask Emily the reason for the moustache. Emily loved the way Isador didn't wear a bra and didn't care, those casual, perky boobs. Emily wanted to repeat aloud how Isador said "horrible" — "oreeble" — but didn't. She thought it all unbearably cute and half want-ed to hug Isador and half punch her really hard.

"No, seriously, but I ask, why? You do not seem to be the Parisian type."

"Honestly? I got tired of following my boyfriend around the apartment."

"What a horrible thing to say." ('oreeble)

"No, no, it wasn't like that, we were both doing really well. He was in a legal firm; he was doing really well. He looked so good in the morning, in his suit. He smelled like lemons and chamomile tea. I was being trained to be an HR what'sit."

"HR?"

"Human Resources."

"What is that?" (What is dat?)

"We hired and fired people."

"Ah." Exhale, tap, twist, twist.

"I was just a terrible girlfriend. I slept, I think, with almost all his friends. I don't know for sure, but I think he knew and he stayed anyway. I made him cook most of the time. He just loved me. For. No. Reason. I couldn't get over that; it sort of made me sick. So I would follow him around, half confused by him and half worshiping him. I'd find his towel hung so perfectly or his boxers folded in the laundry hamper. He would fold his dirty clothes. We would be having sex…"

Isador looked up, blew smoke.

"I mean SEX. Banging against things, rolling about, but I'd look over afterwards and see that — somehow — he had managed to fold his clothes when he took them off. My stuff would be in a jumble; my panties still in my pants, my shirt inside out, my bra god knows where and there was this little, folded neat pile of clothes."

"This is bad?"

"No… but… yes. It made me feel unworthy of him, which is such a stupid-ass let's-turn-evolution-back-100-years thing to say, but I couldn't compete. I didn't want him to find out I went to the bathroom. I didn't deserve this nice boy who looked so good in his suit, who smelled so nice, who fucked so nice, who made the best pesto pasta salad…" Emily paused and then said, as if far away, "We used to fit together so well, from behind, it was like we were molded…"

"So, this boy was perfect so you left him?"

"Well, I didn't really leave him. I just left. I didn't even write a note. I asked my mom to call him but say she didn't know where I was. He's a non-smoking vegan, he'd never think to come to Paris."

Isador lit another cigarette.

"I need more wine, do you have any money?"

Emily was under water trying to open her eyes, her hair swirling black around her like kelp. The room was filled with yellow and orange light from the candles. She had been in there for more than an hour, smoking, drinking gin and swilling the ice in the bowl beside her that was now mostly water. Far off her cell rang. Emily surfaced and reached for the glass of gin sitting on the toilet. Her cell rang again. She listened to its chirping then said, "Fuck!" No one in Paris knew her number so it could only be one of three people, all of whom were in different countries. She got out of the tub, steaming in the cold, and walked naked and dripping into the living room where she'd dropped her bag. She looked out at the building across the street, half registering that if she could see people eating dinner, as she could, they could see her standing naked answering the phone. She hunched down beside the couch. The display was blank.

"Fuck!" Pause. "Hello?"

"Emily?"

"Hello?"

"Emily?"

"Who is this?"

"Hello?"

Static. Traffic. A siren on the phone echoed eerily within the apartment, whoever was calling was in the street below.

"It's your sister, I'm here."

"*Shut up.* How did you… where did you come from… *WHERE* are you?"

"At the front door. It's cold. Let me in."

"No." She said and hung up the phone.

Her sister, Rose, fished out the last cigarette and lit it from the end of her current one. She was sitting on the floor with Emily lying beside her. In the centre of the floor were three empty bottles of wine and a plate with a lit candle melting in the middle of it. In the candlelight Emily thought that she had never seen her sister look more lovely, the dim light softening her drawn, tight face.

"Last cigarette," Rose said, and after taking a drag and exhaling passed it to Emily. They had been drinking and smoking constantly for hours and neither had asked the other the questions they had wanted to ask.

"You had that sweater ten years ago in high school," Emily said.

"So."

"So, don't they pay opera stars?"

"I'm not an opera star, I only sang in one opera."

"So why are you here."

"Can't I visit my sister?"

"Not in the sweater you wore in high school."

Late autumn and the wind made the remaining leaves in the black trees shudder like cellophane. The Seine was an icy, gunmetal gray and thoughts turned imperceptibly from hot drinks to suicide. Emily awoke with her sister's toe scratching her eye. They had both slept on the couch, though Emily had no idea how they managed that. She sat up and for the first time in years, looking at her older sister with her hands curled and twitching in her sleep, felt such tenderness she thought she'd cry. Rose had lost weight; her shirt had ridden up and Emily could see her ribs.

From her apartment Emily could see the river. She stood on her toes and looked down into the street. Not much was stirring save the *patisserie*. The city twisted and turned like a once-loved garden frequented by homeless people.

She was hung over from all the wine she drank and the cigarettes she and her sister had smoked. She truly felt ill. She decided to go out and a rude blast of icy wind hit her full on as she stepped into the street. It made her eyes water. She hadn't a practical coat and was wearing three sweaters, mittens, black pants and big black boots. A tired woman wearing a fur coat walked a small dog to the post in front of her building. The dog sniffed the air with disgust, squatted and left three perfectly shaped, steaming turds on the sidewalk. The woman and the dog moved on.

The city was being rained upon with a gray sleet. Rose, rattling a tambourine she had picked up off the floor, turned and looked at Emily who was sprawled on the couch, reading in a pool of yellow light cast by the apartment's one lamp. "I've now not known him longer than I knew him. Do you think he tells stories about me, getting things wrong?"

"Stop thinking about it," said Emily.

"What's in this?" Rose reached for the notebook Emily had been writing in.

"Don't touch."

"What?"

"They're songs. I'm writing songs."

"You write songs? Can I see?"

"No. You can't."

There was a knock on the door. It was 2 a.m. and the sisters were sitting on chairs with headphones on, playing with an ancient tape recorder and a children's barnyard toy. "Were we too loud?" Emily whispered, looking at Rose.

Rose shrugged and padded to the door. Peering through the peephole, she said, "There's an elegant, rumpled-suited man holding an elf at the door." She looked at Emily, "Should I open it?"

"No!"

Rose slid the chain on to the door and opened it a crack, "Yes?" she said.

"Forgive me," the man whispered in a gorgeous, sleepy English accent. "I heard tambourines and thought I would try my luck." The small girl in his arms shifted.

"This is Sophie. She won't take her elf-ears off."

Rose bent a little at the knees and opened the door to reveal a middle-aged man with a surprise of black hair and tired, tired eyes, wearing a black suit with a white shirt open at the collar. Emily, dressed only in her camisole and underwear, let out a high pitched squeak and ran to the other room.

"Ah," said the man, "and I am Edward."

"Were we too loud?" asked Rose, standing aside just enough to let him slink through the door; he had to pivot to fit in with his sleeping daughter.

"Loud? No, though up until about an hour ago Sophie and I were out." He kissed Sophie's head. "Little pumpkin." Taking in the room and the instruments scattered about, he said, "Are you musicians?"

"Musicians? No, not really. We are recording songs my sister wrote."

"Ah, well." He walked over to a harmonium Emily had brought home the day before and played softly with one hand. "Harmonium," he said then stiffened. "I am sorry, there was a point. Gin. Would you happen to have any gin? Three ounces would do…and a soupçon of vermouth. Sophie has just fallen asleep and it has been a frightfully long day and I've got such a craving for a dry martini and, well, the shops are closed and…"

Emily stepped back into the room, now wearing maroon cords and a purple t-shirt that said 'I (heart) Soup.' The man turned. "My manners. I am Edward. This sleeping bundle is Sophie. We live across the hall, when I am in Paris. Well… I live across the hall. Sophie is visiting."

"Is she yours?" asked Rose.

"Partially. The other part belongs to my wife… ah… ex-wife. I'm uncertain who owns which part, but for now I have her whole. For now." He paused and kissed the child's head again then looking up, pushed back a lank of black hair and smiled. The skin around his eyes wrinkled like soft ripples on a stream and Emily, transfixed, smiled back at him falling instantly, hopelessly in love.

"Imalee," said Isador, "your sister is so bootiful."

Rose wound through the tables with three tumblers of wine, sat down and smiled. "What were we talking about?" she said then lit a cigarette.

"I was telling Imalee how bootiful you are."

Rose scrunched her nose, "Is that accent real?"

It was chill and gray. An intermittent wind rustled the fallen leaves while cats of every conceivable shape and colour scurried between the gravestones. What struck Rose the most was its enormity; so many graves all so elegantly laid out.

"Who is Oscar Wilde?" asked Sophie, twisting and turning her hand in her father's.

"He was a poet and a writer. Irish. Very clever," Edward said.

"Is that a sculpture of him? His dick's broken off."

"Sophie, don't say 'dick.'"

"But you say dick all the time."

"But I don't mean it in reference to a man's member. You never make reference to a man's member unless it's coming at you, but…ah…," and Edward paused. "Let's just hope you won't have to deal with that for some time."

"Member?" asked Sophie.

"Let's change the subject," said Edward and turned.

"Are you a musician?" Rose asked and Emily punched her. "What?!" said Rose, "Cow!"

"Yes, of sorts. A musician. I am incognito at present, a father in Paris raising little Sophie. You might not have heard of me and that is fine." A group of teen hippies holding guitars straggled by looking for Jim Morrison.

"Fuck man, isn't that Edward Pole? Edward Pole, FUUUUCK!" They walked over, shifting their guitars and extending hands, "Dude, the chicks you've had."

Edward winced and smiled. Rose noticed a slight hardening in his face, "Quite. Be careful of that guitar, it may go off."

"You've got that right man, fuuccck, Edward Pole. And Oscar Wilde. Man, too cool! Hey, look, we're look-ing for Jim, do y'wanna come with? Smoke some weed? Commune?"

Edward smiled, "Ah, thank you but I am conducting a little tour with these fine Americans and we must press on. Do smoke some…ah…weed for me."

"You hear that? Edward Pole told me to smoke some weed for him. Too cool! I will man… my man," and the hippie thrust his hand again at Edward.

"Yes, well, keep to the path." And they were off.

Edward paused, looked down at Sophie, "Fans," he said. "Now, let us seek out Héloise & Abélard." They walked a while in silence. Sophie ran ahead kicking the piles of leaves, gleefully singing to herself. Edward broke the silence, "Emily, what brought you here to Paris?"

"Boys. A boy."

"Ah, and Rose?"

"Opera."

"Opera? The Paris Opera?"

"No, no, I was a singer... in the chorus... in Milan. I left."

"Sophie, off the grave, that could be you one day. Would you like someone jumping up and down on your stomach?" Sophie looked at him, then, seeing the logic, jumped off and skipped back towards them. "May I ask why you left?"

Emily, who had been watching her boots scuff the path, looked up. At last, it took a stranger to finally ask the question that Emily could not.

"For a million reasons. A boy, sort of. A girl. The director was a prick who kept burping garlic at me. The bathrooms smelled of dead mice. The city... Oh, I don't know, it wasn't right. It wasn't..." she paused and blew out steam into the air. "I didn't... when I sang, nothing came out of me. Just notes. Does that make any sense? I couldn't understand what I was singing. Not the words, I knew the words. I couldn't understand the passion. I don't know anything! I haven't lived at all! It was like high school there, boys snapping towels and everyone gossiping. I missed my sister. I had wanted it all to change. If I moved somewhere, was somewhere else, I could be different, would be different. Things would change. But my suitcases are still full up. It was just me somewhere else. I don't think blood is thicker than water but finding someone who trusts you is more valuable than any diamond, and more fragile than glass."

Sophie, concerned with the mounting solemnity, hugged her father's leg bringing them to a halt. "I think you are wiser than you know," Edward said. "To hear the words you are singing, you have to stop thinking about them; they are sounds that echo out …" he then stopped himself and looking down at Sophie, said "Are we becoming serious?" Sophie silently nodded. "We have become serious, young ladies, shall we continue our tour?"

"Who're Héloise & Abélard?" Emily asked

"Ah, love. Lovers. This is Paris, come with me."

Sophie tugged on her father's coat, "What, pumpkin?"

She whispered, "Those people said the "f" word."

"Yes they did, Sophie. Savages, savages."

They were drinking red wine and eating potato chips and Vienna sausages out of the tin, Rose on the couch, Emily on pillows on the floor. It was dark and silent with the only light cast by one candle in the middle of the floor. Rose fished a chip out of the bag. "The potato chip," she began, "was invented in 1853 by George Crum. He was black."

Emily reached for the wine, "The things you know."

"It hurts sometimes." Rose reached out, flexing her fingers like a little girl for the wine bottle. "These chips are terrible; my whole face feels greasy."

Emily shifted on the floor, "Will you go back to Milan?"

Rose drank from the bottle, put it down and thought. "I don't know. I don't think I can now. They are very angry with me. I called Mother from the Amex office and she said that Mr. Dalgoise had called and was so angry he shouted in Italian for an hour."

"Poor Mother. That must have been funny. What will you do now?"

"I don't know, stay here… if you'll let me."

"You'll find a boy and leave again. Whenever you are in love you are someone else."

"That's not true."

"No, you're right. You don't become someone else; you shut down everything that isn't about the boy. I hate that."

"Is that why you didn't talk to me for a year?"

"It's not like I had the opportunity. There were some times when we didn't even know where you were!" Emily suddenly felt the bitterness well up. She breathed in the chill apartment air. Outside an ambulance sped by crying 'wheeouuuu' 'wheeeouuuu.'

A large orange cat slunk into the room, tail straight up, a fusty footstool with four stocky bowed legs. It made a beeline to the chips and raised, with some difficulty, a fuzzy mitten at Rose. "Looks like you've had a few too many. Where's Camus?"

"Camus is here somewhere, hiding. He doesn't like this cat but I can't send him away. I think this is his apartment. I think he was here first. Rose?"

"Emily."

"Rose?"

"Emily."

"Rose?"

"Fuuuuuuuuucccccck!" The cat put its ears back and hissed. Rose threw a chip at him and he scurried after it.

"It really hurts."

Rose looked up, "What does?"

"When you just leave like that. I never know when I'll see you again, I feel betrayed."

"Hey, hey, it's not like we're going out. We're family."

"But I trust you, I don't trust people." Emily yelled angrily. "I tell you everything and then you just fuck off for some boy and don't tell me where you are and when you do, you won't answer the phone…"

"Emily," Rose slunk down on to the floor and took Emily in her arms. "Emily, I'm your sister, you have to let me go sometimes. Look, according to Mother, you did the same thing to your boyfriend."

Emily looked up enraged. "That's different. He was just a boy!"

Emily played the piano. She had it rolled into her apartment by a man named Mr. Philippe, who lived down the hall and had offered it to her. Mr. Philippe wore a white t-shirt and baggy black pants held up with suspenders, a wet, unlit cigar in his mouth. His baldpate shone with oil, made shinier by the thin rim of jet-black hair that circled the lower half of his head. "This was my daughter's," he said grunting it into the room. "We bought it for her in the sixties. Sylvie, my daughter; she was at the Academie. So gifted." He grunted, straightened his back then strained into it again. "What was that, that Canadian Glenn Gould? He came and played; my Sylvie says she will never play again. I wanted to sue somebody. Who is this lanky man in his suit knocking the joy out of my Sylvie? So I went the next night and saw him play. When

I came home I said to her, 'maybe an accordion would be better, eh?' "

The room was empty. Rose was out at the American Express office, hoping their parents had wired them some money. Emily played quietly. She hadn't played since she was twelve and it felt unfamiliar, yet comforting. The lamp cast a yellow light. The ivory keys were yellow also. The wood smelled of a thousand cabbage dinners and lemon wood cleaner and cigars. She felt Sylvie's touch on the keys; the electricity of her creativity and the emptiness when she realized she was only average, 'Like us all.' The pedals stuck a little. The huge orange cat climbed in on the windowsill. Night fell and the windows turned black and reflected the room. Emily watched herself play, almost not recognizing herself in the reflection, stiff-backed and skinny. It made her cry.

"What was that?" asked Rose looking up from her book.

"It's the little man leaving milk outside my door on his way to work."

"Does it happen often?"

"At least once a week."

"Do you pay him for it?"

"I don't even know who he is."

"That's weird."

"I know."

Rose got up and padded barefoot to the door. She looked through the peephole. "He's gone." She opened the door and took in the milk. "The bottle is so cute." She peeled off the wrapper and took a swig, "Oh, god, this is all cream."

"Only on the top. Honestly Rose. You have to get out more."

"Sorry. Where I was, milk came in a box."

Camus raced in and wound himself around Rose's leg. "Obviously you are familiar with this," she said to Camus. "Do you give him any?"

"A little, pour it in his bowl."

There came a knock on the door. Emily squeaked.

"What!" yelled Rose.

"It's the little man," whispered a worried Emily

Rose walked to the door. "I'll see." She looked through the peephole, "I can't see anyone." Another knock. Rose swung open the door and there stood Sophie.

"Hello pumpkin," she said bending down.

"I have to go home and I don't want to."

"To your mummy? You don't like your mummy?"

"No, I love my mummy but she always says such mean things about Daddy and I get all sad and she gets all sad and I want to tell her about what we did and saw and she just gets angry at me and then gets drunk."

"Poor precious, I don't know what to say. People are funny sometimes. They don't mean to be cruel but they get so lost in their own lives they forget they are responsible for others. Did you have breakfast?"

She shook her head 'yes.'

"Does your daddy know you've left the apartment?"

She shook her head 'no.'

There was jam on her nose. Rose reached down and took her fragile, sticky little hand, "Let's get you back before he worries. You're very precious to him and he'll be worried if he can't find you. Don't let what your mummy says bother you though I know that's hard. One day, it will be better."

"Promise?" Sophie looked up expectantly and for the first time in Rose's entire life she felt her words weighted down like stone.

"I promise."

He walked ahead not really paying attention to much. Emily was struck with the desire to hold onto him like a child. He seemed larger now, here in the street, than he did as her rumpled neighbour. The cold night air pushed on their faces. The night was indigo blue; the city lights afforded few stars. Cars sped by recklessly. There was a light dusting of snow and in the distance the *Arch de Triomphe* glowed like a stage prop. She caught up to him. He wasn't walking fast; he just took long strides. "Do you miss her?"

"My wife?" he said absently.

"Sophie."

"Oh, Sophie, I miss her, yes. Every day. Hour."

"How often do you see her?"

"Not often. I have visitation rights and whatnot but being abroad…it's hard for her. We don't want to disrupt her school, her …" he trailed off.

"She's such a neat kid."

He smiled, still walking, his head down. "She is, yes. So is her mother. I love them both dearly."

"Can I ask…?"

"Infidelity, infidelity. And really, being on tour. I was the absentee landlord of their love. When Sophie was conceived I had been home for eight hours and was leaving again in 24, not to be back for six months. I was selfish to marry. Possessive. Obsessive."

They walked on. The cafés were filling with early evening drinkers keeping warm in the soft electric glow; the glass fogged, a faint hint of vicious Gauloises. She was enjoying being with him, with his quiet, unspoken dependence on having her near. As they pressed on, her feet began to ache from the cold and the pace that he had set. Suddenly he stopped and turned to her. "Where are we going?"

"I was following you."

"I was walking assuming you'd tell me if I was heading in the wrong direction. What are we doing here? Weren't we going for dinner? There's nothing here for us to eat." He sounded sad. She looked at him and saw a man who had spent his entire adult life an alien. Never settling down. Knowing he could always just leave when things became complicated.

"Let's get a cab, my feet are killing me."

"Oh, I am sorry. With Sophie gone, it usually takes me days to become human again. Here," and he expertly hailed a cab, which slowed to a halt in front of them, bumping against the curb like a gondola. He opened the door and she hopped in, springing on the seat and sighing into the warmth. The driver turned in the seat, "Mr. Pole. Where shall I take you?"

"La Chat Noir, la Chat Noir."

The taxi driver smiled. "I will take you there directly. Hold on please, tonight we are bound for Babylon." And they sped off into the night.

They did not speak in the cab. He looked out the

window, as if taking in the city for the first time, not exactly sure where he was. Each time a street lamp illuminated him, she was struck with just how lovely and weary he looked. He held her hand on the seat and she felt her stomach flip. She knew it was an absent gesture for him, gentlemanly — making sure they got to their destination safely, but for her, she felt as if she was about to fuck her best friend's foxy father.

When they got to the restaurant the driver refused his fare. "No, no, Mr. Pole. That was on me. Thank you." And he sped off.

"Do you know him?" she asked.

"I have never met him in my life. That happens a lot though. It embarrasses me."

The room was packed with patrons and smoke yet they were seated immediately. The whole of the place glowed amber and after the chill night air it felt over-heated and cramped, the table arrangement haphazard. The red-papered walls were striped and festooned with etchings and photographs and sconces spaced throughout with red shades made of tiny fezzes. She had a huge smile on her face; she'd never been happier, she thought. That mixed with 'I've never felt dowdier'. Edward looked over the wine list and smiled back. "You are smiling. Are you laughing at me or happy to be here?"

"Oh, happy to be here. I haven't made one decision so far and at every turn everything becomes more pleasant."

"Ah, well, without a rudder we shall proceed. Order anything, I am loaded." Without a gesture the waiter came and took the wine order. "Forgive me, you did want wine?"

"Of course!"

"How old is Sophie?" she asked.

"Six, she is six this June."

"She's so smart. I liked her a lot. When she came to our door yesterday she said she didn't want to go home."

"Ah yes, well, we go through that every time. Unfortunately my wife… ex… my ex-wife goes through a day or so of grief each time she returns and takes Sophie with her. We love each other still, I suspect. Like the ghost pain of a missing limb." The wine was brought and poured reverently. When the waiter left he topped the glasses to the brim. "Fuck niceties, I want to be drunk. Oh, sorry, if you don't mind."

She raised her glass, "I'd have it no other way."

"My wife was a model. She's very aloof and incredibly smart, much smarter than me. When we married I knew I had years of hard work just to bring myself to the point where I could be of interest intellectually to her. Why she married me, I could not fathom. I suspect it was my celebrity."

"Stop that," she said then stuffed some bread in her mouth. "You are fascinating."

"When I keep silent. I don't know. I fall in love quite easily. So much is said about me because I did so much. I used to think that was a badge of a life well-lived. Now it bores me. I wish I were a baker."

She felt indulged, indulgent. "Tell me about places you've been."

"No, you tell me," he smiled and leaned forward. "You are the exotic one. You and your sister, recording at night, I am fascinated and so jealous that you haven't asked me to even shake a maraca or bang a drum."

"We're too self conscious and in our egotistical way maybe we don't want to use anybody else. I think half is because we don't trust anyone and half is because we don't want people to see how incompetent we are."

"Nonsense. I'm sure it's charming. May I hear some of it one day?"

"If you're good."

He put his hands out in supplication. "I can promise nothing."

"Did Mom give you my number? It's so late here and I just got home... No... No... Sometime, not yet.. I have money... I do... Nothing. Stuff. I'm recording a record... It's true. Rose is here... What?... No, here... She went over the wall... What?... She hasn't said... I didn't ask her... Robert, Robert, are you crying? Robert?... I'm sorry... No, sorry... I know you love me... What?... No. No, it wasn't like that...I'm sorry. I just thought... No, you're right, I didn't think... I didn't want to hurt you... It wasn't selfish... I didn't... Robert... Robert... Stop! I'm sorry. You're just so nice... No I know that's not a bad thing. I know you... What?... I know, but I can't. I don't want to. I want to live here... Paris... It doesn't matter... It doesn't matter... I can speak some, but it doesn't matter... No, I don't want you to come. No... Did Mom tell you that? What did she say?... No. Robert... Robert... It's not that I don't love you, please don't cry. I just couldn't be what you wanted. I'm no good at it. I'm not nice... I know, I know. Shhh. Shhh. I know, I know... I don't want to write letters. Responsibilities? But you were my only responsibility. Honest... Who said that?... Who?... I don't even know this person and you're worried about what they say?... But that's just dumb office stuff. Who cares?!... But why?... Robert, I love you. This is how I show it. Why do you so want me back? I can't play the part. I was slipping up. Every day it was getting more and more intolerable. I tried Robert, I really tried. I wanted to be the little housewife... I'm sorry, I know that's not what you wanted, but... I meant it metaph... Robert. Please... Robert, I can't. I can't come home. Please stop asking. I felt like I was playing a part. Like any second someone would walk in and lift the carpet up and find all this dirt there. My dirt... No, it's not about getting a maid. You're missing the point... Robert, please, can't you see? If you really loved me you'd see that it'd be best for you not to be with me. I'm not very good at life. Real life. Or someone else's life. The real world life stuff... So I ran away. Staying made me miserable... Ok, so you were happy, but I was miserable. You didn't notice?... You didn't?... What?... I'm so sorry Robert, I love you. I can't be with you. You're too nice for me... No... No... No... I'm sorry... Please... Robert... Please... Let me go... Robert. Robert. Are you there?... What time is it?... Really?! Shouldn't you be in bed?... Why are you sleeping on the floor?... Since when?... Oh Robert, please, I feel so awful... What's that sound? Is it raining?... I know... I know, under that awning thing... Robert, please, I have to go... Please don't call me again... What? Ask mom. I talk to her... What?... I don't know, maybe... No. Please. Don't you see? Find someone nice... I'm not nice, I left you Robert, haven't you noticed?!... I'm sorry... No... Look, it's four a.m. here. I have to go to sleep... I'm sorry. I'm going to hang up... For real...I'm hanging up now... Robert?"

Click.

"I love you."

Mr. P and Mrs. Z

"A HOUSE BY the sea, a house by the sea, how lovely your view is," sang Mrs. Z, staring out the enormous window. Mr. P was in the shadows furiously shaking a martini shaker.

"Yes, it is a wonderful view. Sometimes the fog rolls in from the sea like a great wall, or a ghostly hand about to smother the land. Sometimes one can see ships and can imagine one's self sailing off to exotic shores."

Mrs. Z paused. "The sea actually terrifies me but for some reason I always feel so much better when it is near by."

Mrs. Z had arrived not twenty minutes earlier. She had finally made an appointment to interview Mr. P, his reluctance to grant such an encounter propelling her on. To get to Mr. P's there was long drive through a dense stand of evergreens, its scent rich with nature alive and nature decaying. Above the sky was blue, yet in places the trees were so thickly clustered hardly a shaft of sunlight pierced through. She walked the path, humming to herself, feeling at peace and content inside. A cloud covered the sun and the air instantly chilled, then the sun burst out again and warmth streamed down. She paused and put out her arms as if to capture it all, her feet shifting in the fine dust of the path. In the forest she imagined spider webs and moss. As she got close to the house, she noticed an old bicycle had fallen on the path. She picked it up and began wheeling it towards the entrance.

Mr. P himself greeted her at the door. He was dressed in a loose white dress shirt, his tie slightly undone, his shirttail hanging out. His spectacles dangled on a chain around his neck and his dark gray trousers had dusty patches on the knees. He looked like he had been working in the garden.

"Forgive me. I heard the clock chime," he said, holding open the door from inside, "but I have been so lost in moving boxes to and fro I feared halting the momentum. Were you ringing long?"

"My dear Mr. P," laughed Mrs. Z. "I have just this instant walked up your drive!"

"You walked in from town?"

"It isn't far really and it is such a lovely day to be walking. Is this your bicycle? I found it lying on the grass and thought I'd move it for fear someone may trip, leaving you open to lawsuits…scandal…broken bones…ruin!"

"Oh dear, I must have dropped it when I came back from my evening ride. Mr. Flowers generally keeps an eye on my lapses," he smiled, "but today is his day off. I fear you will have me all to yourself. Is this quite proper?"

"Well, maybe not proper, but…" Mrs. Z smiled as she

leaned the bicycle against the stone wall where it sank a bit in the rich earthy moss.

"Please, come inside," motioned Mr. P.

This was Mrs. Z's first formal entrance into Mr. P's world, from the riot of birdsong outside to the ancient cloistered silence of the house within. The hall was narrow with a mirror on one side and single line of eight small watercolours on the other. The pictures were very faded, with hints of trees and landscapes. "They were by my mother," said Mr. P, noting her interest and taking her coat. "I'm afraid this house is still, after so many years, a mystery to me. I cannot, despite my attempts, bring any more light into it. I am unacquainted with its original owner but I sense he was a mole, or perhaps someone who earned his living underground. Save for the windows in my study, which drift out to the sea, every window seems to have been placed at a disadvantage to the sun. Come…" and he extended his paw, "how nice, despite what I know of your mission, to have you here. I have always felt we two were the outsiders in our little corner of heaven."

"How so, Mr. P?"

"Well, everyone in some way… no, I guess I am connected to our lovely neighbours to the west…I'm not sure," he paused in thought. "I feel you and I…we are the shadow workers. We two do not let a lot…we do not surrender… we do not…"

"We keep our secrets to ourselves."

"Well yes, that is a way of putting it."

They moved on. The hall led into a large, strangely shaped antechamber.

"Perhaps the original owner really *was* a mole…or an ant. What a curious layout for a house," said Mrs. Z.

"I've often thought ant farm," replied Mr. P.

She counted seven doors. "Oh dear, Bluebeard's Castle!"

Mr. P was leading her to the farthest door. "I had never thought…goodness, you are right." Each of the doors was made of oak; the walls were covered in a dark green forest of wallpaper leaves and twisting vines, and now and then the red stain of a poppy. Under the numerous carpets, the floor was parquet with rich ebony and white woods.

There were half circle tables pressed against the wall — one by each door — containing flowers in various states of decay, bones and butterflies under glass, numerous brass ornaments and bells, Hindu gods and incense burners.

That's it, thought Mrs. Z, Mr. P's curious underscent. Incense! It lingers in his fur. How she would love to press her face into the thick fur on the back of his neck.

"There," said Mr. P pointing to the various doors, "is the kitchen, the hall to the east wing, the bedrooms, the library and my studio. Over there is the entrance to the west wing and this, the seventh door, is my study.' Above each door Mrs. Z noticed a brass plaque in an arcane language. "I have yet to translate them all," said Mr. P, adjusting his spectacles. "They are in Old Dutch, which excites me as a number of my mapmaking heroes spoke that language. This one for example, the one above my study, this one says something of the room by the sea…

wait…" he whispered, quietly trying to phrase it, "literally it says 'drift now away, the sea will…' Oh dear, I cannot quite make out that word. I have lived here how long and still have yet to master Old Dutch. Where are the scholarly Dutch persons when you need them? Shame on me!" He laughed to himself and placed his paw upon the latch. "This is my most favourite room." Pushing open the door they were greeted by the lovely afternoon sun which flooded into the antechamber, warming its old bones and filling it with that unmistakable smell of the sea. Mrs. Z breathed in deeply.

It truly was a spectacular room. There were enormous windows on the far side giving an unhindered view down the lawn to the sea. French doors opened onto a terrace and the top of Mr. Flower's cottage could just be seen near the forest's edge. The curtains billowed lazily with the breeze. There were large fireplaces at either end of the room with a dusty mirror mounted above each one, carefully positioned to reflect the other. As it was a warm day, no fires were lit and in the grates sat huge fire screens, peacock-shaped with tails spread. Each mantle was held in place by two colossal figures, and the tops were littered with all manner of bric-a-brac: marble heads, carved birds, marble balls of all sizes and colours, boxes that held curious bits of taxidermy, and strange jars filled with a viscous fluid containing what looked like asparagus floating about. Mrs. Z 'pinged' one with the tip of her finger. "Sea asparagus," said Mr. P proudly, "Quite rare."

The floors were mostly taken up with carpets, though now and then patches of dark wood peeked through.

Innumerable couches, all sunken and beyond inviting, sat amongst low tables laden with books, sculptures and tangled plants of all shapes and sizes. To her amazement, mounted along the entire wall on one side of the room, were hands: waxen doll hands, tiny and delicately painted; crude prosthetic hands, articulated and stiff; artist's dummy hands made of wood and metal; automaton hands, pathetically reaching out as if for alms; baby's hands; men's hands; women's hands; hands of the aged. "A fetish of mine — hands," said Mr. P shyly. "Please find a couch to your liking and I will, if it is not too early, fix us a cocktail."

"Oh, I cannot imagine one not to my liking," said Mrs. Z as she threw herself upon a faded Victorian sofa that faced the open windows, a small cloud of dust rising. "This is perfect. Oh my!" she shouted, noticing the ceiling of black and white striped canvas. "Is that tent material?"

"Yes. Queen Victoria," said Mr. P, seriously measuring liquids, "or so I have been led to believe anyway. She had it with her while in India. I like to think of her sitting underneath it beside the Indian Ocean, the dangerous Indian night sky above, while I sit and contemplate my own bit of heaven and the sea."

"How wonderful. How splendid this all is. It will be most difficult concentrating on our conversation with so much to distract me."

Mr. P laughed from the drinks cart behind her. "I can't imagine my conversation containing anything really that could be of more interest than any one of the objects on this room. Perhaps rather than writing about dull me — and really, we must talk about this — I could give you an inventory of this room's contents. The list alone would be of greater interest…" and he shook the cocktail shaker loudly to drown out any protestation. Walking around, he laid a silver tray on the table before them then gently sat himself down onto the couch. Mrs. Z had an enormous and contented grin on her face, her feet upon the table and her arms outstretched along the back of the couch. "I have never felt more comfortable, thank you."

Mr. P on the other hand, nervous of the interview, was stiff. His motions were deliberate. "I do hope you like this. Gin and lychee liquor. I haven't named it but it does…well…hit with precision. Oh goodness, have you eaten? With Mr. Flowers gone I had supped off cold things in the pantry. Shall I make you some toast and jam?"

"Heavens Mr. P, I am perfectly fine. You forget I have a daughter. If there is anything that happens in my life with any sort of regularity, it is meals."

"Ah," he said. "Now drink this quickly. Its flavour diminishes with each second it warms."

The glass froze the tips of her fingers like an icy fire. She took a small sip — delicious — then a huge gulp. An enormous gray-bottomed cloud passed in front of the sun causing the light to dim drastically and the edges of the cloud to glow all yellow and then white. "Oh, this is lovely," said Mrs. Z.

Mr. P sipped his drink. His nostrils quivered and the long whiskers above his eyes twitched with pleasure. "Yes. I cannot contradict you." They sat in silence for a brief moment watching the cloud above the sea. It was all so perfectly still. One could just discern the sound of seagulls and the gentle crackle of the tide receding below the cliff, the scent of the just-cut lawn and, now and then, honeysuckle or roses.

"Another?" said Mr. P.

"Oh yes, please!" said Mrs. Z.

Mr. P shot up and behind to the drinks tray. "I am working today left to right with my cocktail mixes. Like words on a page. Let us see how far we can go."

"Indeed." Mrs. Z brought her feet down and reached out for a book half open on the table. "Are you reading Whitman?"

"Well, somewhat. Mr. Flowers quoted something which I was sure was Whitman and we have been hotly debating it ever since. Where are the English scholars when one needs them?"

"Obviously in cahoots with the Old Dutch ones," Mrs. Z laughed.

"Well, yes, and I fear now it could actually be Keats and I am not prepared to travel down that road quite yet," continued Mr. P, furiously shaking the cocktail shaker. "Now, try this," he said, slipping back upon the couch. "Chartreuse, green. And beware, take this one slowly."

"Oh dear," Mrs. Z coughed, "this is pure alcohol!" It burned icy in her throat, but deliciously, as the tips of her hair follicles tingled. "You, Mr. P, are trying to get me drunk so I will forget my mission here."

"I have forgotten your purpose already and had hoped that you had just come simply to pass a pleasant afternoon," sighed Mr. P. "No? Well then, what honestly could possess you to want to write a book, or base a book, or even consider me — *me* — interesting?"

"No, that is not how it starts." Mrs. Z put her glass down. Her lips tingled and tasted deliciously of sugar crystals. "We cannot start on the negative."

"Well then, ask away." He reached out and poured the remaining pale green liquid into her glass. "There is a passage, wait," and he got up and went to the far bookshelf.

"Not fair. Not fair. You've prepared! You've made notes!"

"No, no, but I did re-read your book the other night, you may call that preparing." He came back to the couch and sat down — again that haunting smell of incense. He looked at her. She was flushed, "Oh, does this make you uncomfortable? I am sorry." He ran his hand upon the book. "Are you not," he said touching the volume, "proud? You made this. There are thousands of copies exactly the same. The same words moving people in different ways. Isn't it startling?"

"But Mr. P, your maps, your charts. Ships at sea are finding their way because of you. It is just as magical."

"But does one look at my map of say, the tip of Gibraltar, and hear the voices of the people there? Do people come away changed as one does from your fiction? Are they reading between my lines? Goodness, actually, I hope not! I wouldn't want to inspire a ship to run aground. I am literal, my dear. You are literary. You are the ghosts that lurk. I am...I am..."

"You are becoming drunk."

"Well yes, another?" said Mr. P.

"Yes, maybe…"

Mr. P got up, took her glass and retreated gingerly to the bar. Mrs. Z looked at the book. She knew it by heart, but had not looked upon it in years. There were sections that were painful to her, and she still felt she had not gotten it right. There was so much more she could not put down on the page. She had laid herself bare. She had opened a love letter in a crowded place and read it aloud. She cleared her throat.

Mr. P returned with fresh drinks. "I've wanted to say since first I've met you, tragedy wears well on you. It has brought the inside out and has made your eyes quite luminous and lovely."

They both sipped their drinks contemplatively. For the first time Mrs. Z heard a clock ticking. They both stared out at the sea changing colour with the dusk now approaching.

"I have a secret, Mr. P," said Mrs. Z, finishing off her drink and putting her glass out for the next.

"Vermouth, lime cordial and gin. A secret?"

She drank the drink in one gulp and leaned forward towards him, placing a serious hand upon his sleeve. "I play the trombone."

Mr. P began to laugh and spilt his drink upon himself. Recovering, he wiped the excess gin off his trousers with a mannered gesture. "Well…and now keep this to yourself," he leaned towards her whispering. "I have an absolute passion for passementerie." And they both roared with laughter.

Despite Mrs. Z's quick eye, she had not noticed the tassels and cord, fringe and frog, lying, waving or hiding about the room. "Were you aware," Mrs. Z began, "that the wheel used to twist the silk into cords…"

"…was invented by Leonardo Da Vinci?" interjected Mr. P.

"Damn, my only tassel anecdote."

"Now if that does not end up as a delightful entry in someone's autobiography I do not know what will. Another?" said Mr. P reaching out for her glass.

"Goodness! Soon I will lose the use of my legs."

"We have a whole evening to regain them. I can try my hand at making us supper later on," laughed Mr. P from the drinks table. "Ah, here, now try this. This is something I'm sure you've never had. Lavender."

"In a cocktail?" And she sipped the icy liquid. How strange the taste — like stepping off a train in a tiny sun-baked station in the south of France, the arid Provençal air sweeping in and clinging like hot salt and sand to your skin then suddenly, a chill breeze with that delicate scent of lavender.

"Lovely," murmured Mrs. Z. "This reminds me of a candy I craved as a child. My aunt used to make it for me, delighting I think, in the fact I loved something that all the other children abhorred. I cannot remember its name now. I seem to remember it being French." Her eyes drifted as if she were scanning pages of a familiar book. "Mr. P?"

"Yes, my dear."

"Lycanthropy?"

"Yes, Mrs. Z?"

"What do you… no…how does it…well…When you hear people talk, or in books, does it interest you?"

Mr. P got up and walked to the window. He looked so comfortable here in this room, thought Mrs. Z. He was much taller and stockier than she ever assumed, his demeanor condensing him somehow; a gentle giant. How careful his actions were. His movements choreographed like a magician — she saw him as a boy in front of a mirror practicing. There was a joy to it, a love of the steps, a subconscious ballet of sinew, which pulled the drapery back so elegantly.

"Lycanthropy amuses me as a minstrel chorus must amuse a native of Africa. A whole history turned into ignorance and insult."

"Your family," said Mrs. P.

"My family?" Mr. P stiffened.

"I have neglected to ask, do you have brothers or sisters?"

"I had a family, yes." Mr. P stared out the window. Solemnly he spoke, "A mother, a father — wonderful, kind people."

"Wolves?"

"Well, yes," he laughed quietly. "Of course, wolves."

"Oh, do forgive me, I only…"

Mr. P waved off her embarrassment. "Forgive me, Mrs. Z. Yes, they were wolves. My family — mother, father, brother, sister — like anyone really. They were quite brilliant, or I thought them so, so much more than I. One year," he paused sniffing the air, his back to her, his eyes fixed on the view. "One year a very brutal but influential man did something absolutely unspeakable to a child," Mr. P closed his eyes as if to shut out the memory that pained him. "Horrific." He paused then turned to Mrs. Z. "Word began to circulate that a wolf had done this. No one was certain who started the rumour, or on what fact it was based, but they needed someone, something, to hang this violence on. Certainly no human could do this, no person could be so vicious…so disgustingly vicious as to take that child, someone's daughter, and translate her, first to an object of desire and then to a nightmare of murdered flesh." He slowly shook his head, then quietly, methodically, continued. "My father was a milliner, a maker of hats. My mother painted watercolours. My brother was going to be a brilliant linguistic, I think. My sister," he smiled and breathed in, "my sister… she didn't know what she wanted. Her eyes were the most beautiful of blues. I think she would have been a writer." He turned back to the window. "I was away at college you see," he said quietly, "I didn't know until I got back…our house… my family…I had a family, Mrs. Z. They were culled."

Silence.

"I am so sorry," said Mrs. Z sober suddenly.

Mr. P recovered. "The past is past and I cannot bring them back." Drinking the dregs of his martini, "I must keep moving, trying to have what was good in them live on through me. To live," he waved his hand in the air, "move towards the ones you love. Now, forgive me Mrs. Z," he chuckled. "Is this the kind of thing that makes a juicy novel? We should go see if Mr. Flowers is back and while we are walking, we can talk of trees."

"How delightful," said Mrs. Z, grateful the subject could be changed.

Mr. P smiled and still clutching his glass, he invited her out onto the garden lawn. "You know the origin of the word *lunatic*?" asked Mr. P, holding back an errant clump of ivy that had grown across the doorway, as they stepped into the garden.

"As a matter of fact," said Mrs. Z, pausing to breathe in the heavy lilac scent, "I do not."

"To be struck by the moon. It was believed at one time that one could be struck quite literally — or perhaps more wonderfully, metaphorically — by the moon. It drove one mad. And I suppose it would," he chortled.

"I should think it would hurt, actually," said Mrs. Z.

Mr. Flowers Talks to the Dead

A Secret Chapter

THE DEW SHONE silver in the light of the rising moon. The warm evening air was thick with perfume, the dryness of the dust on the road, the sea salt spray — almost a shock after the cloistered rooms and the softness of the house. They breathed it all in, the alcohol in them making it that much more intense, as if they were falling backwards into a liquid air. The scent of the night blooming stock delighted them, pouring down to the very bottom of their souls then up and into their heads, almost making them tipsy again with the pleasure of being alive this night. Mrs. Z kicked off her shoes, as suddenly she needed to feel the wet grass between her toes. "Promise me…Oh…" she steadied herself against Mr. P, "…I do not forget my shoes."

"A gentleman, Mrs. Z, makes sure his companion leaves as she came, her clothing intact."

"Mr. P," laughed Mrs. Z and punched him gently upon the arm.

"Shall we visit Mr. Flowers?" asked Mr. P. "I know he is about. Perhaps he could freshen our drinks," they clinked their glasses, "or at least offer us some tea." He gestured, holding out his arm. Mrs. Z took it, feeling so incredibly happy, so warm and safe. The wind whispered through the dangling tendrils of the willow trees. "Willows are notorious for trapping spirits. Were you aware of that, my dear Mrs. Z?"

"I was not."

"Oh indeed yes. Occasionally Mr. Flowers and I will come out with brooms on nights such as this and ruffle the branches. We must be quite a spectacle, but it has to be done. I will have no roosting spirits in my garden!" Mr. P paused, then said, "The ancients thought the earth-god...everything...every aspect...was presided over by some deity. It was believed," he waved his hand, Mrs. Z on his arm striding beside him, "and I believe it still, trees have souls. It was considered practically murder to cut one down, a sentiment that is certainly lost now. The North American natives sometimes attributed their defeat and decay to the fact that the Europeans leveled their forests, the spirits that protected them from harm rising with the dust into the sky. In the Molucca Islands, blossoming trees were treated as if pregnant, which I suppose they were...pregnant with fruit. No noise could be made near them, nothing was allowed to mar their slumbering ancient peace. In Amboyna no loud sounds were allowed near the rice in bloom lest it should turn to straw. Why, the ancient Gauls worshipped trees of a certain sacred forest and the Druid priests of England revered mistletoe of the oak holy. Such a pleasant ritual that." Mr. P seemed in his element, thought Mrs. Z. What a wonderful teacher he would be, his voice low as if sharing a secret long kept in a dark, warm attic room. "The veneration of trees, springs, rivers and mountains is the oldest traceable religion of Asia. Many mountains were holy places. Earthquakes were the gods shrugging their shoulders. Flexing. Turning over in their sleep. Everyone, everywhere, at some point knew the importance of the earth. Why in fact, 'matter,' the Latin *materio* and *mater* 'mother,' are so close. Why have we forgotten…Oh, dear, forgive me. I am going on. Am I boring you?"

"On the contrary Mr. P," replied Mrs. Z, "I was lost in your words. I was actually thinking of the spirits trapped and tangled in your willows, wondering if there were any there tonight. How sad it would be for them if they could not come out and walk with us or feel the wet grass between their toes. These cocktails…are there cocktails like this in the afterlife I wonder?"

"I should think they wouldn't be needed. I should think the afterlife, heaven if you will, would be glorious."

"Like right now," said Mrs. Z, nuzzling into Mr. P.

"Just like right now," answered Mr. P. A pause. "Gracious Mrs. Z, I must remember to speak of trees more often."

They walked a bit more, crossing the gently sloping lawn, the crickets and frogs and peepers echoing in the forest while above bats tittered, darting busily to and fro. "Ah," Mr. P exclaimed as they came to a small stone path leading towards a small storybook cottage with a thatched roof; its windows spilling out yellow. "Mr. Flowers is at home. Did you know that William's parents recommended him to me? They had met him at a séance where he confessed he was tired of travelling and was looking to settle somewhere. He has been my assistant ever since."

They were still quite tipsy and walking on the uneven stones was difficult. Mrs. Z. stumbled, spilling what was left of her drink; laughing, Mr. P caught her elbow. "In his off-hours he convenes with the astral plane so we must be quiet as we approach," cautioned Mr. P. "Lord knows what he may be up to or who he may be speaking with."

Just then, from within the cottage, there came a huge crash that sounded as if a whole pantry shelf had been upended. "Oh damn and blast!" shouted a voice from within. A red face appeared in the window. "Now look here, whoever you may be…" then realizing it was Mr. P, "Oh, I say Mr. P, and is that Mrs. Z? Oh I am sorry for my French," he said embarrassed. "Dear…please… ah…Won't you come in?" and he quitted the window and suddenly appeared, opening the front door for them. "I'm afraid you will find my place a tad untidy. I was making great headway with Mrs. Madeline Woertman-Pynn."

"The late temperance-league woman?" asked Mrs. Z.

"Yes, the same. We were having a grand old time. She was levitating my flow blue about the room. You see it now," his voice lowered, his arms outstretched, "shattered upon the floor." Mr. P and Mrs. Z stepped inside of the cottage into a low and open room that had a large fireplace with a large copper kettle and rotisserie set in. Two ancient wingback chairs faced it. There was a long wooden table and a sideboard covered with flowers, photographs and numerous clocks, none of them ticking. There was, as far as Mrs. Z could make out, no electric light. All illumination was coming either from the low burning fire or candles set into the whitewashed walls. The stone floor was littered with a thousand shards of flow blue china. Mr. Flower's sighed, "I did love that set."

"Oh my dear Mr. Flowers, what happened? Was there static?" asked Mr. P.

"No, Mr. P. You remember Mrs. W-P and her temperance work? It seems she brought it with her from beyond the grave. She sensed there were two people in their cups, shall we say, and left in a tiff."

"Oh, I am sorry," laughed Mrs. Z. "That is dreadful. The least I can do is help clean up."

"It's alright, Mrs. Z. A visit from my living employer and a quite lovely, very much alive author more than makes up for the pottery shards and the hasty retreat of Mrs. W-P. Now, what were you two up to on a night such as this?" He leaned forward like an indulging schoolmaster.

Mr. P picked up an empty bottle of gin, which had been hidden behind a stack of books. "Oh dear Mr. Flowers, you have gone dry."

The Girl In The Box

EVEN WITH THE last rays of autumn light spilling in, the room seemed dusky and cold. The curtains billowed gently, the breeze making the pages of the book left on the side table flutter like startled birds. The room smelled of cleaner — lemon, but harsher; the maid must have left the window open. Removing her hat, she hung it on the back of the chair and kicked off her shoes. She dropped her bags on the floor and threw her purse on to the freshly made bed, where it bounced then sagged. Outside the city slowed and relaxed its shoulders into evening.

The skitter clickity-clack of the owner's enormous dog passed in the hall; the echo of a latchkey; the cold tile floor; the sense of loneliness. It grew dark quite suddenly and she moved to the window to shut out the chill. A romantic hint of autumn rain was in the air, there, almost invisible amongst car exhaust.

In a country where she didn't speak the language, the greengrocer thought her simple. Despite all her traveling, she found nothing was ever easy or charmingly foreign (and thus comforting). The English newspapers only reminded her she was far away; the poor English of the restaurant menus depressed her. Only the saints seemed understanding, their hands folded or waving gently, blessing her in a sort of stony absolution from high above on the church walls. They said, she hoped, "You are loved."

Her dress was simple and black. She pulled it off and sat on the bed in her underwear, too tired to do much else. She dumped her bags, spilling out books and cards, buns and chocolate and cheese, museum brochures, rolls of film, various boxes, arcane charms, an ornate saints medal, a candle and a small cobble stone. She raised the stone to the light, "Did an exiled pope once tread upon this ancient smoothness?" she thought and raised it to her nose to smell. Creosote. Stone. The candle she put by her bed.

She struck a match from the box she had pocketed from a café and lit it. The room turned orange then yellow. She hadn't noticed how menacing the armoire looked and suddenly blew the candle out, fanning the smoke away nervously.

By the candle was a letter, which arrived that morning at the hotel. She recognized her mother's distinctive handwriting on the blue airmail paper, the dipping spidery letters in black ink. It had been mailed two weeks earlier. This, too, she held up to smell but it smelled of nothing; not of the sea or her father's cloviness or the wooden floors of her house or the rain outside on the garden. It smelled of paper and of its travels — in bags, in planes, in trucks then up these stairs. She put it down, deciding to read it with dinner.

Her arms were sore from carrying her bags and her back ached from museums. She had a rash of red between her breasts. She decided her legs needed to be shaved, but she couldn't be bothered.

She went to the washstand and removed the grime that had come from being out of doors all day. In the harsh glare of the bare light bulbs that surrounded the mirror, she looked tired. Her black hair made her skin look yellowish, not pale. The deep green of her eyes were faded; her lips thin. She rummaged through her purse for her passport and remarked at the difference with the girl in the photo — a young girl of twenty with jet-black hair and piercing intelligent eyes.

In the hall she heard the couples locking doors, heading downstairs to dinner. Children squealing. Running. She steadied herself as the first thunderclap of the promised evening storm came.

She walked back to the bed and reached for the black box she had bought and forgotten in a sea of tissue. The girl at the store said it came with a story and showed her the hidden latch with the spring mechanism that opened it slowly as if underwater. The box was inlaid with thin gold metal, some now missing, but finely detailed and spindly. It looked like the kind of box a magician would have owned and let no one touch. The girl said it had come from a woman who was selling off her husband, bit by bit.

The shop girl spoke perfect English and carried herself with the confidence people have in the presence of those with none. She made breathtaking eye contact — as if she had been waiting all day for the girl to come in.

"It's German," she said, "see, on the bottom. We can find no reference to it in any of the books we have, see." She pushed the latch and the lid slowly moved up. Inside was the tiny ivory figure of a girl, lying on her stomach on some sort of daybed draped with an elaborately carved throw. Nude. One arm fell off the couch and on to the floor, the other seemed to be under her. "Some sort of erotic clockwork, see," and she pushed an unseen button and the figure slowly arched her hips — just slightly — then brought them back down.

She had never seen anything like it before. It really wasn't something she would have been interested in. The box was, however, incredibly beautiful. It also had a strange eeriness to it and an energy that made her feel that she was meant to buy it.

"It's odd," the girl went on, "I don't really like this side of curiosities, the pornographic one. But this little hidden girl inside this beautiful box," she rubbed her finger along the miniature back and face, "I feel sorry for her, isn't that strange?"

The store was beginning to overwhelm her with its Victorian clutter: bejewled eyeglasses; glass tableaus of extinct fowl and rare fauna that had been lovingly laid out; croquet sets; bowler hats; elephant foot umbrella stands; surgical instruments; boxes of petrified bees — nothing dating past 1910. Arcane mementos, asleep with their secrets.

The shop girl didn't even smile when she bought it, treating it all as if it were a matter of course. She took up one of the store cards and wrote her name upon it. "My name is Emily, this is my number; I live alone, you can call. I know you are visiting, perhaps we could have dinner or I could show you what I know of this city."

She flushed as she took the card and felt a bit weak in the knees. No one, boy or girl, had ever been so forward.

Sitting now on the bed, she retrieved the delicate card and placed it by the candle and the letter. She ran her hand upon the box's arcane smoothness. It seemed cold, dead; a casket for the ivory girl inside. Another crack of thunder and suddenly all the heavens poured down upon the ancient and now empty streets.

Fireflies

LATE NIGHT AND fireflies flit along the path, their light fading in and out like candles guttering in the wind. The trees on either side of the road moved silently in the warm sea air, themselves a sea of rich fragrant dark greens. She thought, 'I should be afraid,' as her bare feet padded upon the soft dusty road. She heard crickets and frogs and in the distance a cow lowed; near was the sea. She paused and put her arms out, the warm air rushing over and around her, her hair flowing out behind.

The fireflies then encircled her, so many for such a night. Perhaps it was her stillness; perhaps they sensed something collectively, not wanting the moment to pass unmarked. They landed on her arms, in her hair, in the folds of her shirt, their glow random and soft. She wanted to slip off her clothes and just stand there. She wanted rain to come, cool and forgiving to wash everything away.

It was not so much the exhaustion or the scratches covering her bare legs that then overtook her, it was the fear; a fear that followed her unseen across the fields and had just stopped here in this familiar landscape. Standing between rows of ancient trees, she cast her head back to look at the sky and fell — still standing — into a deep cataplectic sleep, what she feared more than anything else, a waking sleep. Her body then gave way and she crumpled on the sand in the middle of the road, sending the fireflies into the air like sparks. Animals hesitantly came out of the shadows. The fireflies floated down and gently crawled their way back into her hair, her clothes.

The scent of blood on her was overpowering.

And always the sound of the sea.

It was that rusty scent that he caught first, pedaling towards his house in the dark on his bicycle, the forest path changing constantly with the moonlight and the night. He had driven this route so many times, loving it best like this, on his bicycle, as the night closed in with shadow and became another world altogether.

The air, however was making it difficult to pedal.

A sudden gush of warm air carried with it the sickly sweet smell of blood. The scent was overpowering — absolute and final. Blood, fresh, too fresh and too near. His nostrils quivered, taking it in. There was nothing in these forests he knew that could generate such a strong scent. Overhead, the quick flutter of bats. He became overcome with foreboding. He knew he was not in any danger, he just dreaded what he might find ahead and as he thought this, rounding the corner, he saw her. Or rather, he saw something. First it was a glowing shape lying motionless in the middle of the road — an apparition perhaps, a trick of the light. He stopped his bicycle, the ground beneath his feet feeling unexpected and hard. He let his bike down gently. "Dear God," he whispered, not exactly sure of what he was seeing. The fur on the back of his neck bristled, his ears twitched as he approached. The phantom shape was still glowing, illuminating the ground around it. He knew the animals were close by, watching — the air was thick with their worry. He salivated, disgusting himself.

His night vision was weak after years of work, and because of the years themselves, but he could see it was a girl, a girl covered in fireflies. "Hallo?" he cautiously said aloud, his voice suddenly unfamiliar to him. He edged closer. She was alive, he could tell. As he moved closer to the circle of light he realized the scent, the odour, was coming from her. He knew her. "Oh dear God, dear God," he felt faint and overcome. He reached out; a hiss arose from the forest. He touched her, almost vomiting from fear. "Oh my poor child," he muttered, close to tears. He touched her shoulder, her cheek warm. "Oh thank God," he sighed and smoothed her wet black hair back from her forehead, noticing her eyes darting under the lids. "Oh my God, what has happened?" He ran his hand along her side, feeling her solid presence, trying to discern any damage. Her heart was racing. The fireflies were filling her pocket, moving in and out of her hair. He tried to shoo them away. His hand touched her skirt and recoiled. It was soaking wet with blood, deep wounded blood, that metal smell mixed with helplessness and fear, turning the dust black on the ground. Hunched beside her in the glowing light Mr. P threw back his head and howled uncontrollably. It came from deep inside him; an overwhelming pain for this girl whom he loved like a daughter, asleep and broken here in the road. This was unbearable to him.

His hands then moved down her legs, the cuts from the brambles already scabbing. Splashes of mud, the soles of her feet black, her toenails broken and caked with earth. Tears came, so full and burning. There was nothing in him anymore that knew how to deal with this emotion. He had thought himself long immune, almost dead inside, but suddenly he was back in a room he had not entered in ages and every memory was still as sharp as a knife. "My poor child. I know you are there, I know," he choked on a sob. "Oh God, I will get you home. I will get you home, don't worry." He gently brushed her hair with his hand, dispersing the fireflies. Kneeling, he reached under her, wincing, her body so fragile, this girl he'd known almost all her life now crushed and asleep and covered in blood. He cradled her gently then rose up. "Everything…" he sobbed, "…everything is going to be alright. Oh dear god," he cried.

They were near to his house. He would take her there first, just until he knew what was wrong. He would send word round that she would be staying with him as he could not let William see her like this; it would be too much. He began to walk with her in his arms. Her shirt bloodied; the scent was intoxicating. He swallowed, his tail out straight behind him for balance. "I will take you home. I will take you to my house, would you like that? It will all be better soon." The certainty of that he did not believe.

The stars had shifted. He knew the animals were following. He wasn't sure how long she had been there or for that matter how long he had crouched beside her. He was scared that he had waited too long, too overcome with emotion when time was precious. He couldn't tell the extent of her wounds and worried perhaps he should not have moved her. He knew that she was coherent although asleep, turned within herself. He must talk to her. He knew that.

"I loved your father. I found life in college with him wonderful, liberating. I had never been with someone before who was so focused. You could have been a postman or Madame Curie, he did not care, you were either interesting to him or not. I missed that when school ended. I'm sure you know his ability to cheer whomever was in the room. He could charm the birds out of trees. Whatever you said to him, he made you feel it was the first time he had heard it and it was the most exciting thing he'd heard all day." Why was he telling her this? He felt a chill coming through the forest. He knew he was close to his house. "After school I knew I had to make a name for myself but I am…well…not easily acceptable to all. I needed a place away where I could work. Establish myself."

His voice was breaking; this was too much. He had to resist the impulse to lick the wounds on her legs. It was unbearable. He stammered on, "I was fortunate. I had money. I could go anywhere." He felt the blood seeping into his shirt; his hands under her were soaked through. He took a breath. "I managed to find a place which suited me perfectly. Outside it was tumbling down with boxwood hedgerows and a sad, sad topiary of elephants and bizarre pieces of hunt-shaped shrubbery — the horses melting into the lawn from neglect while a leaping fox blended into the garden wall. When the doorknob fell off in my hand, I knew it was for me. There was solitude there. The queerest thing, however, was the house itself. It measured ten feet smaller on the inside than out. What I loved the most was that it had a decaying swimming pool, completely encrusted with weeds, roofed over by a glass conservatory that had been added onto the back. I knew this was where my studio should be. It was like a hot house for me to plant and grow my future. There I would nurture whatever it was I was meant to be. I lined the walls with bookshelves. I took my drafting table down there. I could look up and see shrubbery horses racing with elephants on my lawn."

He could see his house now, he could see lights on at Mr. Flowers' and was grateful for that; he would need someone with a level mind to calm him. He continued, "I had enough to hire on a cook and I managed to engage a woman who took no notice of my appearance whatsoever. I remember her saying, 'I think I've seen enough of life to say that I'm not shocked easily. However, if you don't eat all that I make for you or if you ever come into my kitchen complaining of salt, then you'll get my notice!' I'll never forget her red hands and severe black hair tied so tight she squinted." Her breathing was slowing; did she know where she was? "Stay with me please. It's not too much farther," he said, choking back tears. His legs ached and his clothes stuck to him from sweat and her blood. "It's just here. We're here now, dear God." He reached out to the door, jostling her slightly, her body still not stirring. "Stay with me. I cannot suffer to lose you. Please. Not anyone else."

Mr. Flowers rushed in, wondering about the disturbance. Mr. P raised a finger to his lips for silence. Their eyes met.

"Oh dear God," whispered Mr. Flowers

They quickly drew a bath and placed her fully clothed into the steaming water. She stirred, a slight moan, her clothes shifting like sea vegetation.

"Is she conscious?" asked Mr. Flowers.

"She is asleep and I pray she remains so," whispered Mr. P, his stern face focused on the girl, his arms immersed, holding her up. He thought of Ophelia as her dress buoyed and turned the water a pale pink. A rose. There was still the unbearable scent of rust. "I found her in the road." There was a worried pause as his eyes met Mr. Flowers and words failed. "No," stammered Mr. P, reading his friend's thoughts, "I do not believe she has been…"

"Tampered with." Mr. Flowers breathed.

"The blood seems to be from the wounds. I fear she has run through the brambles and got cut up quite badly."

"What could have caused her to do such a thing, to run through them like that?" asked Mr. Flowers.

"She came from the eastern forest." Mr. P shivered. "There are some places just so evil and horrible, they produce the strangest of howls."

Lost at Sea

SHE SAID HER name was October as that was when they had pulled her from the sea.

It was the tank I remember the most, that along with the briny smell, and the rust, the cold, and the green sickly light. They rarely changed her water and so she just floated there in her particle sea; her only hope was the hope of dying. She said her name was October as that was the month that they had found her. She had been hauled out of the sea, caught tangled in a net, gasping for air. She never told me her real name; she said it wasn't important.

I had stayed in that town lacking any alternative, my grief hanging upon me like a badly worn suit. The tourists had gone home and the air grew crisp, filled with the smell of burnt leaves and roasted chestnuts. One night just outside of town along the river, a street of carnival tents magically appeared. Shabby ill-tended rides were run by even shabbier carnies while sad and woeful strippers stood on raised platforms looking disinterested and cold. Under the unsympathetic white lights that had been haphazardly strung up like a constellation of drunken stars, barkers called to us with tales of the night and its infinite mysteries. At the dreary end of the midway was a long tent fronted by a tattered banner pocked with holes. Inside, it boasted, was a live mermaid.

The crypt had been flooded since the 17th century. The sea wall broke and water poured into the tunnels and crypts dug by the Romans centuries before. There had been no attempt to drain it or to patch the hole that led out to the ocean so it became an eerie subterranean grave, and later, a tourist attraction where for 25 centimes you could illuminate a few green, murky feet and peer into its abyss. Word had spread that a mermaid had swum in and the church became a place of pilgrimage. The holy fathers were grateful and never said a word.

I brought her there as I knew the water to be salt and that she could survive, however grim, and maybe even find the tunnel to the sea. At least it was better than being in that tank. She lay on the floor of the rented car swathed in a wet sheet, shivering, passing in and out of consciousness, talking to me when she was awake, moaning softly when she was not.

"October, it's not much further," I said.

I had worked it out as far as the abduction, the rented car, the key (she told me where it was hidden), the sheets to be soaked. I had the map, the torch, warm clothes. I was also drunk, out of my mind on nerves and vodka.

She weighed little as I lifted her out of the tank, her fierceness reduced to utter fear as I laid her down on the trailer floor and she heaved and shivered, waiting for me to soak the sheets and cover her with them. I wrapped her as best I could and she began to cry. I filled a bucket full of the tank water and then as an afterthought, dumped my thermos of coffee and filled that as well.

As I picked her up off that hard cold floor I thought never had I felt such sadness; it radiated out of her. She was now entirely at my mercy and she held me so tight she nearly winded me. Her tail was unbearably slimy and covered in mold, like picking up a slug. Her skin, however, was dry like suede. Her breast flattened against me. She looked up at me. I tried to smile.

I cautiously opened the door, confirming October's assertion that the carnival did indeed fall over blind drunk at 2 a.m.

I propped the door open and carried her to the car that I had parked behind the caravan. When I got the door open I slid her into the back seat, dousing her with the bucket of water, not even thinking of how I would explain that to the rental car agency.

"Hurry," she whispered. Already her lips were chapping. I climbed into the front seat and sped off into the darkness, the spinning wheels of the car kicking up gravel and flinging it against the trailer. Of course a dog barked somewhere but no one woke. I swerved then righted and regained control. I was so unused to driving; being drunk and in a foreign country didn't help.

"October," I shouted to the back seat, "Do they drive on the right or left in France?"

"Francis William," she said quietly, "I am from the sea, how would I know?"

In my panic, I wasn't even sure if I was headed in the right direction. I ploughed down the road into the darkness, a lone car on a highway that cut through a field of grain. The night was pitch; there was no moon, the lights of the car were virtually ineffective. This was the ancient autumnal night we drove in, where spectres wait at darkened crossroads and mist steals the souls of little children.

She was beautiful, elongated and fair. She would change colour from a pale green to milky tea. She had black eyes with no whites, huge shoulders and small breasts. Her fingers were webbed. Her hair was long and tangled with seaweed. She would circle her tank, hitting the sides pathetically then drift to the bottom where she would sit, her unblinking eyes staring out of the glass, burning with rage.

I went back every night. I would place my hand against the glass and whisper. She heard me, at first just glancing at me then slowly growing used to me, becoming less guarded. She placed her hand on the glass, an inch apart from mine.

"Seven screws hold the tank together," she said. "Seven nails hold a coffin shut," she said. "They think it will ward off evil."

Slowly, in pieces, she told me her story. How she became entangled in a great drift net, the kind commercial fishery boats use. She passed out from being dragged with it for so long, the screams of the other animals and fish trapped there with her, unbearable in the darkness of the sea. She awoke in a holding tank on the fishery vessel, sick. She had no memory. She vomited often, which floated in the water along with bits of whatever they had stored in there before and cigarette butts that the crew had flicked in. There was no light, no one came, no one brought her food, she thought she was going to die, she thought she was already dead. She told me she was afraid of the dark.

The captain sold her to a collector who smuggled her in a van to a loft where she stayed for the better part of a year. She hardly saw the collector except on those days when she would awake to see him sitting naked in a chair in front of the tank, furiously masturbating. One day another man came and injected something into her and when she woke next, she was in that tank, in that trailer.

She spoke with an Irish accent; she said it was Welsh. She didn't know how old she was, she didn't know where she learned English. She was so full of bitter rage it was palatable. She never asked me who I was, just my name — Francis William.

I leaned over the side of the boat; the water was boiling with activity, catching the moonlight, turning the water white. In the turmoil swam October. She circled and looped beneath me, a graceful shadow in the dark water. I leaned further to see her more clearly and she suddenly shot up and grabbed hold of me, pulling me in.

I thought I knew how to swim but I lost all my coordination. My arms were useless; I thrashed and thrashed but got nowhere. She came up under me and pulled me cascading into a tunnel of bubbles, away from the boat, away from the surface of the water.

She held me in her arms, "Trust me," she said, and I let go, I gave myself to her. I became still, I let her take me down into the blackness of her sea.

I wasn't sure when, but I realized I was breathing under water and I laughed.

There was light all around us, light from a thousand million phosphorescent sea worms, wriggling like dust caught in a shaft of light. I watched the tiny bubbles escape from October's nose. The oxygen escaped through the pores of her skin. I lost myself to her; I acquiesced.

She stopped and let me go. She began pulling off my clothes.

We floated there, under the water. I noticed then that she had legs. She wrapped them around me; I felt her muscles, her strength. I could do nothing. We kissed violently, she pushed so hard, our teeth hitting. She pushed herself into me, bruising me. Her hands were on each side of my face, her legs held me. She worked herself on top of me and then I was inside her, floating in the sea, glowing in phosphorescence. I had never felt such intensity, as she forced me deep into her. I felt faint. I kept my eyes open, watching her fucking me. Her eyes closed, her face lost. Around us there were dark, black shapes like huge shadows running along indigo walls. Intelligent eyes suddenly, then gone. Soft fish moved around us, seaweed rose and held us. She spasmed, gripped me and we both came. I came in her, in the depths of the ocean. In the glowing living ocean, we floated, locked together, locked together.

Finally a road sign, the church was near.

It wasn't that large, but it was ancient and wet, covered in lichen and rot. Gravestones tilted in its small graveyard. There was a long, low stone wall leading up the drive on one side and an ancient, arthritic row of black trees on the other. The church was silent and dark when I approached it. My stomach was in knots as it dawned on me that I hadn't factored how I was going to get into the church and October down into the crypt.

"Francis William," she said.

"Yes?"

"Why are you doing this?"

"Because you are sad."

"That's hardly a reason."

"It's the only one I have"

"Francis William?"

"Yes."

"If I could, I would love you."

I pulled the car up as close as I could and turned out the lights. I doused October with what was left of the water and left her in the car. It was so cold but she said she didn't mind, just to hurry. I ran furiously around the church, pushing against every door I could find until I came upon a small unlocked one at the side that opened into an empty whitewashed room. I found an entrance into the main of the church and raced to the front, pushing open the doors. There was no alarm, just the sound of the night pressing in and October sobbing in the car. It had begun to rain, icy cold.

I ran out, pulling open the door to the car. I picked October up and carried her into the church. I stumbled and knocked over a rack of candles. I thudded her against pews as we headed for the stairwell that led down into the crypt.

Emily died of cancer. It had started in her breast on her birthday and although they managed to halt it there, it spread to her brain and in the end all that we were able to do was keep her from hurting too much. I spent a lifetime of midnights sitting in her hospice room watching her, holding what was left of her, her brain a haunted circuit board of remembrances. She laughed in her sleep, lucid and alive; she cried; she swore; she talked to her parents who were long dead; she talked to people whose names I did not know. Slowly, memory-by-memory, she unplugged each one then switched off the light and silently died. At 4 a.m. leaving me alone. Five weeks after we admitted her. Six years after I had realized I had never loved anyone so much as I had loved her.

I gave up. I had so few things. I packed them all in a box and left it at my parents. I took what money I had and left on the first flight out of the country. Jet-lagged and shell-shocked, I landed in Paris ten hours after I had taped the last box shut. I told October this as I lowered her into the freezing salt water. She looked at me unblinkingly. The darkness made me faint. I am deathly afraid of dark water.

"Francis William," she whispered.

"Yes."

"If you set me free you will never see me again."

"I know," I said.

"Thank you."

I could barely see her in the darkness. She swam out, gaining strength, taking in huge breaths of air and water. She went under and I thought she had gone, but she appeared again right by the steps.

"Francis William, what is this haunted place?" she asked.

"My goodbye."

She dipped under the water and then was gone. Ripples lapped against the slick, black stone and curled around my shoes. I held my hands to my face; my fingers smelled of rust and salt. I sat there, freezing, on the step until I could barely feel.

I thought how I had left the car door open in my haste to get October inside. I thought of how everything I owned now was stored in a box. I thought of how sorrow had taken me to this far-off land where I had been presented with a magical gift that I could not keep. I grew intensely bitter then profoundly sad. What are these gifts we are given and why are they timed so and why are they always taken away?

I have so much love to give yet I am never given the chance to see it through. If I could do anything, I would take away the sorrow. I would not be afraid of the dark. I would follow the currents out to the middle of the ocean and find October. I would hold her close to me, and I would tell her stories and I would never let her go.

The Vervain

THE VERVAIN TOOK advantage of the high tide, and with the urgent pull of the moon, slipped silently out to sea. Aside from the dull thrum of the engine and the creaking of the cabin woodwork, the girl was enveloped in a delicious silence. This particular crossing was so under-booked that all third class passengers were moved to second so a half crew could be employed. As luck would have it, she had a room to herself. Two rooms actually, and a bath. The books of transatlantic crossing etiquette had not prepared her for this floating church of manners and she felt awkward and quite alone. The hallways were lined with shoes at night, which she took as some sort of custom of not wearing one's shoes in the cabin. In the morning, along with a tray of breakfast foods, she found her Mary Jane's by her door, lovingly polished, looking newer than they ever had.

The room smelled of dust and soap. She'd never been in a darker space although she had two portholes, which looked out to the sea and a rich milky sky. She was able to open one using the huge brass nuts and screws, and when she did, so rich was the smell — the lovely dead alive smell of the sea — that it seemed as if all of the ocean in one gust slapped her unsuspecting face and nearly pushed her across the room.

Outside her room, the ship had its own smell of cooking close by, coffee all the time, over-bleached linen and unturned-out rooms and sleepers; like a hotel that had been set adrift at night. Yet this hotel did not sleep. It was magical and alive and there was always someone, alone or in pairs, wandering. Stumbling. It was like Venice letting go of the pretense of being attached to land. She had found her room early but only to toss her bags in as she did not unpack. She twirled once when alone, then twice, then three times, then remembering to lock the door, ran to the aft deck to witness her past trailing away.

Was she too young to be doing this, as her mother had said? She pulled the sleeve of her sweater past her hand and put it to her mouth, breathing warmth into the wool. She thought, 'have I begun an adventure, or made a terrible mistake?' She reached into her pocket and found a letter there.

"My Darling," it began in her mother's hand. "Despite all that I've said, and the caution that I've given you, I know you will be reading this one midnight on the deck, or in the cabin of a ship. I know what is pulling you away from me, and I must not think that it is infinite, this pull, that it will weaken and cease and then you will come home to me. I made you the headstrong survivor that you are, and now I must let you be that. Know that I love you more than anything I can imagine. I feel at times I could burst, and thinking about you now…."

She folded the paper back up and stuffed it in her pocket. She was not ready for the rest. She turned to the horizon. One small tear rolled down the side of her nose and into her mouth, and then suddenly, an avalanche of emotion, shaking, making her bend in a spasm of grief. What had she done? Who was she hurting? Her resolve, the business of the trip, everything had kept her mind occupied; but now, staring at the immensity of the sea, the future weighed down upon her and made her feel small, like a tiny letter in the middle of a very long sentence. She slid down onto the deck, pulled her knees up to her chest and cried. Passengers circulated by her like ghosts. A young man in a white uniform holding a bouquet of paper flowers squatted down beside her. His knee cracked. He pulled out a white handkerchief and handed it to her; it glowed blue in the moonlight.

"We've all these good-byes, Miss. I suggest next time the forward deck for absences. Best to look to the misery ahead of us, than the misery we are leaving behind. Believe me Miss, there will be plenty of time in the long life ahead for that." She blew her nose into the crisp fabric and snorted gently. "Are you a boatswain, officer?" she asked. "I've always wanted to meet a boatswain."

"No Miss," touching an arcane insignia on his sleeve and standing to leave. "I am the First Mate." He clicked his heals and left her.

She never saw the man again, despite the small crew, but she never forgot what he said and in her box of sacred things, beside the ball taken off her bedpost, she put the handkerchief, still damp from her tears — the first tears she had cried at her own insignificance and her ability, despite that, to harm someone who loved her with such enormity it would never cease to humble her.

It was on the second night that she met Mr. Woolley. She had seen him throughout the first full day of the voyage, but had not actually spoken to him — really, would not have had the nerve in the first place, but the circumstances were so odd — and what isn't odd about floating a thousand miles out at sea in a metal boat with china plates to eat upon and a swimming pool, lit like a lagoon listing slowly? It was very late. She had found that despite being very underage, she could secure glasses of champagne from one or two of the indulging barkeeps — and she did. Champagne made her feel so warm and oddly happy. She wandered the passageways, listing with the boat; voices, snatches of conversations, the electricity of the sleeping passengers seeping out from the doorways.

She made her way one deck below, to an ornate cocktail bar where a brassy quartet played listlessly during the evening. Smoke still hung in the room, despite it being so late and the bar since closed. At the piano sat a gaunt gentleman in his black dinner jacket; his collar stud had come undone, but he had not noticed and so one side of his collar had shot up. He had placed a half empty martini glass on top of the piano and was, elegantly and exaggeratedly, playing Satie. His head was stooped forward and he was obviously very drunk. His skin was a pale alabaster, he had a very long, very straight thin nose beneath which sat a pencil-thin moustache. A cigarette dangled between his lips. His hands were long and thin and he had the look of someone who enjoyed the choreography of playing the keys as well as the actual sound they made. His legs were like sticks under his pants, which had a silver stripes running down each leg. The sound of the piano haunted the space.

Without stopping he said, 'I see you, you know. I realize we are our own little country here, far away at sea, but I say, aren't you a little young for drink? Far be it,' he paused and trilled on the keyboard, never looking up, "far be it for me to pass judgment on the demon drink; however, you seem to be quite unchaperoned and so here you are, into your cups, a young waif without a matronly aunt, and you are about to make your first wrong step towards a life of utter misery by talking to me."

He stuck a chord, then sprung to his feet, stretching out his hand. With a list of the ship, he lost his balance and fell to the dance floor. He put his hand up again from the floor, taking hers, "How do you do. How do you do, perhaps you've heard of me, Cecil Herbert Woolley; double U, double O, double L, E-Y. Thespian. Esquire. Sellout. At your service." He rose as if tugged by an unseen puppet-master, made an enormous bow, stumbled back, butted up against the raised platform of the stage and sat down. "Now your name...don't tell me, is —" he put his hand to his brow, "Esme."

"Why, however did you know?" she said astonished.

"I asked the First Mate," and he bowed again.

I Do So Worry

HE PUSHED THE cart gently down the hall, the only sound the shuffling of his bedroom slippers and the chiming of the bottles all neatly arranged on top. Slowly he began to realize where he was, what he was doing. Slowly it sank in that he had no idea how he got there, why he was doing what he was doing or for how long. His faced flushed and his heart raced; he felt utterly, utterly em–barrassed and scared. He quickly pushed the cart to the sitting room and as best as he could and as silently as he could, replaced each bottle back on the sideboard, trying to remember how they had been originally. He stowed the glasses and returned the cart.

He walked into the bedroom and sat heavily on the bed. "My husband," she said from the vanity seat, turning and stretching out her arms. Sensing something wrong she rose and crossed the floor, sitting down beside him. She took him into her arms and he exploded with tears. She pulled him closer, his sobs so violent they rocked the bed but muffled in her dressing gown with her arm around him. She held him like that, waiting, saying nothing, feeling him spasm epileptically, and she listened.

The windows were black with night; she saw the two of them reflected, his hunched figure, her stiff, upright, loving self holding him. When he finished, he lay back onto the bed, his feet still on the floor. She got up and got him a drink of water from the carafe by the bed, making sure he had the glass firmly in his hand before she let go. Their eyes connected. She kissed him. His hand shook as he drank the water. Taking the empty glass, she kissed his hands; they were so brown and spotted now, his nails thick like an animal's. She got on her knees, "my beautiful, noble husband," and put her arms around his legs, holding him. He put his hand on her.

The clock struck the hour, then the half. She looked up and he was asleep.

She went to her writing desk and pulled out a box of cream cards with envelopes and her pen. She wrote three notes quickly in her sprawling handwriting, begging the recipients to carry this knowledge with them, to never tell the children. She sealed each one, addressed them and left them on the desktop.

Pressing him gently, "Get your overcoat, we are going for a night sail, the sea air will do us both good, clear the cobwebs."

He looked at her, "Night sail? But darling I'm exhausted, it's late, can't imagine even crossing the lawn let alone the sea."

"I will help you," she said and gently got him up. Holding him, they crossed the room and went out into the hall, along it, down the stairs and on to the landing.

She pulled her coat on, then helped him with his. She kissed him again and smiled.

Out into the night, the air chill and pressing. There were no clouds, the moon was full and made everything silver and the shadows deep and long. They crossed the lawn, then down the steps to where the boat was moored. She settled him in the forward cabin, mixing him a drink, then went back up and cast off. The moon made navigation simple. She glided the boat out of the sheltered part of the bay and raised sail, leaving ribbons of moonlight in their wake.

When they were far enough out that the lights of their house, and their neighbours, could not be seen she set the wheel and went forward to her husband. He was asleep, holding a thick glass half filled with gin in his hand. His head was back on the cushion. She went to him. She had never felt more tenderly toward him than she did at that moment, his ill-fitting body a rumble of shirts and socks, trousers and suspenders. She pushed the hair off his forehead and tried to stick it back; a small cowlick of gray. She kissed him as she took the drink from his hand and set it beside him. He awoke and blinked.

"I'm afraid I'm not much help, mother, have we set sail? Where to — around the bend then back?"

In the distance buoys clanged.

"I've never loved anyone but you," she said. "I've never told anyone my secrets save you, and I know they are still there." She tapped his head. He looked at her confused, concerned.

"Darling," he said, "it was an incident, one of many yes, but I'm alright, I'll be fine, can still find the loo, that sort of thing." He reached for his drink and winced as it burned in his throat. He coughed violently. She held him again, trying to pull him into her, feeling so much give in his clothing, in his flesh; she wanted to crush him. She buried her head in his neck. In her subconscious, in the house she often wandered, she opened the linen chest and pulled out the quilt that had started when she was born, and laid it out in front of her. It went on for miles, flapping as it unfurled. First it was the gentle pink of baby fabric, the satin ends, the tiny perfect stitches, then the optimistic green and confident double-stitches, the perfect patterns, the breathtaking accuracy. The quilt unfurled on, pushing down into the parts of her house that she rarely visited — where some rooms were left unfurnished, while others were not even painted, the plaster left to dry unattended. The quilt was now gray, unfolding inelegantly, the missed and dropped stitches that couldn't hold the patches on, that were themselves ill matched and poorly planned as if they were just a second thought. The quilt moved on into darkness.

She stood up gently and stepped back. "I love you," he said. "I love you darling," she said.

From her pocket she removed a small pistol that she had had for years. She pointed it at him and pulling the trigger killed, instantly, the only thing she had ever loved. His eyes remained open; he looked at her utterly confused then slumped forward, dead.

She put the gun down and walked towards him. She pulled a blanket out from under the seat and put it over him, knowing how cold it gets at night, at sea. She tenderly tucked him in. She took up the bottle of gin, then turned and closed the forward door, locking it.

In the engine room she rooted on the floor until she found the stopcock and pulling it, let in the sea. It seeped in slowly then quicker, with purpose. She stepped out, closed the engine room door and went on deck. Bringing down the sail, she tied it carefully to the boom then went to the aft cabin where she sat down in her favourite chair. A novel was wedged in between the arm and the cushion. 'So that's where it had gotten to,' she thought.

The launch was now in the southeastern tidal current, which came in warm and silent, just below the icy surface of the sea there. It nudged the boat and carried it out into the darkness.

The sky was starlight.

She drank a long draught of gin, then another, then another; after four she passed out. The launch lowered to sea level and the black water breached the sides and gently poured in, filling the forward and aft cabins quicker than the seacock, sucking the boat down into the warmth of the tidal pull. It glistened as it sank, leaving shimmering sparks from the reflected stars.

At some point she awoke — the sea at that point was tremendously deep and the ship had been falling for quite some time. She pushed herself out of her chair and began to swim. Out, away from the boat. Not a frantic crawl to the surface, but down, elegantly, away from the night. She watched her craft twirl into the inkiness, and noticed lights there, in the distance. She suddenly remembered the strokes of her youth, the Australian crawl and the front stroke; she attempted a few, pleased at her results. The deeper she swam the more clear the lights became; it looked like a whole city. A whole city at the bottom of the sea. If only her husband were here, how he would loved to have seen it.

———————— ◆ ————————

David Keyes was born on an island in the Adriatic Sea, but was raised in a suburb of Toronto. His career in the arts spans almost 30 years and includes musical works for dance, film and stage, literary pursuits, art happenings, curatorships, coffin making, fashion and film.

For your added pleasure…

THE 5 COCKTAILS of Mr. P

As imagined by
The. Rt. Hon.
Richard Shallhorn,
Viscount Inwood

INTRODUCTION

A S I SIT here in the library looking out over the garden under its blanket of snow, my thoughts drift towards summer when our garden becomes the inspiration for many cocktails. Despite the altitude here in "York Est" the garden thrives, yielding a bounty of lavender, mint, basil, rosemary, chilies and other botanicals some of which have found their way into these cocktails. Stimulated by the descriptions in the Mr. P and Mrs. Z I have tried to capture the essentials of the four cocktails mentioned as well as creating a special drink inspired by Mr. P himself while only using common ingredients easily made or purchased and without complex mixing instructions or elaborate garnishes. Certainly feel free to adjust proportions to your own liking and include whatever creative garnishes you desire.

A well-made cocktail is a wonderful thing. By turns relaxing and restorative I will admit to having a few during the Jekyll affair, that curious incident with the giant ape in Manhattan and of course at the end of the hard week of reviewing the estate accounts. But the most enjoyable are often those consumed with friends during the course of a good conversation or beside one's partner on the couch or together at sunset by the shore of one our northern lakes with a good book in hand.

The inestimable help of my wife and our dearest friends, who allowed me to experiment on them and whose feedback informed these creations, is gratefully acknowledged. Any faults with the recipes rests with me alone.

Cheers!
R.S., Lord Inwood

Please find a couch to your liking
and I will, if it is not too early, fix us
a cocktail.

~ Mr. P

INGREDIENT RECIPES

Chili-Infused Vodka
1 - 2 Dried chilies split
lengthwise
1 cup vodka

Combine vodka and chilies in a glass container (small canning jars work well) and let sit at room temperature tasting after 6 hours and then periodically thereafter until the vodka is well infused with chili flavour and heat. Remove chilies and any seeds. Store in the freezer.

Lapsang Souchong Infused Vodka
¼ cup vodka
2 teaspoons Lapsang Souchong tea
(loose)

Combine vodka and tea in a glass container (small canning jars work well) and let sit at room temperature tasting after 6 hours and then periodically thereafter until the vodka is well infused with tea flavour. Remove tea leaves. Store in the freezer.

Simple Syrup
1 cup of water
1 cup of sugar

Combine in a small pot and heat stirring until sugar is fully dissolved. Cool. Pour into storage container and store in fridge.

Lavender Simple Syrup
¼ cup simple syrup
1 – 2 tablespoons dried lavender

Combine simple syrup and dried lavender flowers and store in fridge for 24-48 hours. Taste periodically until a strong but not overwhelming lavender flavour is apparent. Remove lavender and store syrup in fridge.

Mint Simple Syrup
¼ cup simple syrup
6-8 fresh mint leaves

Combine simple syrup and mint leaves. Muddle (lightly crush) and store in fridge for 24-48 hours. Taste periodically until a strong but not overwhelming mint flavour is apparent. Remove mint and store syrup in fridge.

COCKTAILS

Each recipe makes one drink.

For each of the cocktails, simply combine all the ingredients in a cocktail over fresh ice, shake vigorously and then pour into a chilled martini glass

---

No. 1 Treasure of Bihar

1 ½ oz. *Hendrick's* Gin
¾ oz. Lychee liquor
¼ oz. Chili-Infused Vodka or Chili Vodka

No. 2 L'Autre Fée Verte

1 ½ oz. *Finlandia* Vodka
¼ oz. Green Chartreuse
¼ oz. Simple syrup

No. 3 **The Thin Man**

    1 ½ oz. *Victoria* Gin
    ¼ tsp. Dry Vermouth
    ½ oz. *Rose's Lime Cordial*
    ¼ oz. Lime juice freshly squeezed

No. 4 **La Provençale**

    1 ½ oz. *Gin Mare*
    ½ - 1 tsp. Lavender simple syrup (to taste depending on strength)
    ¾ oz. Lemon juice freshly squeezed
    ¼ oz. Simple syrup

No. 5 **The Colonel**

    1 ½ oz. *Bulleit* Bourbon
    ¼ oz. Mint simple syrup
    ½ oz. *Finlandia* vodka
    ¼ oz. Lapsang Souchong Infused Vodka

Acknowledgements

I would like to thank Jean Nielsen for her time, her inexhaustible patience, her wise editorial eye and her kindness, Nancy Baker for her friendship and sage editorial advice, Richard Shallhorn for his graciousness and mixological brilliance, Ray Caesar for his kindness in allowing us to use his haunting painting for the front cover, and lastly Gillian Holmes for her inspiration, love, brilliant design and brilliance in general.

I would also like to thank the people who have magically inspired and influenced me over the years, Rebecca Baptista, Tanya Schreck, Annie Smidt, Diana Obscura, Liisa Ladouceur, Eileen Arnow-Levine, E. Katie Holm, Lynn Crosbie, Dame Darcy, Russell Smith, Magda Trzaski, Christine Stait-Gardner, Deane Hughes, Becky Taylor, Renee Bosler, John and Sandra Huculiak, Daniel Richler, Taeden Hall, The Marlow and its occupants, my family and of course my second family, the Royal Sarcophagus Society.

Colophon

Set in Bembo and
Mona Lisa Solid ITC TT

Bembo is an old style serif typeface originally cut by
Francesco Giffo for the Venetian humanist printer Aldus
Manutius around 1495. The Bembo font used in the text of
this book is a revival designed in 1929 under the direction of
Stanley Morrison for the Monotype Corporation.

ITC Mona Lisa Solid was created by designer Pat Hickson in
1991. It is based on a typeface that was originally drawn by
Albert Auspurg in the 1930s.

ITC Luna was created by Japanese designer Akira Kobayashi,
who was inspired by the Art Deco designs of the 1930s

Designed in 2012 by Gillian Holmes of
The House of Pomegranates Press
and typeset in Toronto on an iMac computer.
2nd Edition 2015